Samuel Bowles

A Summer Vacation

in the parks and mountains of Colorado

Samuel Bowles

A Summer Vacation
in the parks and mountains of Colorado

ISBN/EAN: 9783337287894

Printed in Europe, USA, Canada, Australia, Japan

Cover: Foto ©Andreas Hilbeck / pixelio.de

More available books at **www.hansebooks.com**

THE SWITZERLAND OF AMERICA.

A SUMMER VACATION

In the Parks and Mountains

OF

COLORADO.

BY SAMUEL BOWLES,

AUTHOR OF "ACROSS THE CONTINENT."

SPRINGFIELD, MASS:
Samuel Bowles & Company.
NEW YORK:
The American News Company.
BOSTON:
Lee & Shepard.
1869.

SAMUEL BOWLES AND COMPANY,
Electrotypers, Printers and Binders,
SPRINGFIELD, MASS.

THESE letters of a Summer Vacation, in saddle and camp, among the great Central Parks and Mountains of America in Colorado, are gathered into this volume in order both to satisfy and stimulate the public interest in a region of our New West destined to a peculiar place in the future of America. We saw enough of it in our stage ride across the Continent in 1865 to suggest that it would become the Switzerland of America; Bayard Taylor, a wider traveler and closer observer, made a more familiar tour in 1866, and more formally pronounced the same judgment; and now, after a new visit, and an intimate acquaintance with all its details, we find our original enthusiasm more than rekindled, our original thought confirmed.

The distinctive physical feature of Colorado is her wide elevated Parks, lying among her double and treble folds of the continental range of mountains—great plains, like counties in Illinois and Iowa, or states in New England, six thousand to nine thousand feet above the sea-level, surrounded by mountains that rise from three to five thousand feet higher; plains, green with grass, dark with groves, bright with flowers; mountains, dreary with rocks, white with snow. The distinctive charm is the atmosphere, so clear and pure and dry all the while, as to be a perpetual feeling, rather than vision, of beauty ; invigorating every sense, softly soothing every pain, lending a glory to landscape and life alike, clothing every feature of nature with beauty, and giving the eye of every spectator the power to see it—this is the indescribable thing that lifts Colorado out of other lackings, and more than compensates, in the comparison, for what is peculiar to Switzerland.

Here, where the great backbone of the Continent rears and rests itself; here, where nature sets the patterns of plain and mountain, of valley and hill, for all America ; here, where spring the waters that wash two-thirds the western Continent and feed both its oceans ; here, where mountains are fat with gold and silver, and prairies glory in the glad certainty of future harvests of corn and wheat—here, indeed, is the center and the central life of America,—fountain of its wealth and health and beauty. Switzerland is pleasure and health ; Colorado is these and use besides—the use of beauty, and the use of profitable work united. I beg every traveler by the Pacific Railroad not to "pass it by on the other side ;" for, in so doing, he would offend the best that is in him.

S. B.

SPRINGFIELD, MASS.,
February, 1869.

LETTERS.

COLORADO:

Its Parks and Mountains.

I.

THE PACIFIC RAILROAD.

The Contrast of 1865 and 1868—Vice-President Colfax, Governor
Bross and their Summer Vacation Party—Chicago and the Ride
thither—The Pullman Cars of the West—From New York to
San Francisco without Leaving the Car—West from Chicago—
Council Bluffs and Omaha—Across the Plains by Railroad—
Cheyenne—Up the Mountains—The Charms of Scenery and
Atmosphere—Railroad Cities, their Rise and Fall—How the
Railroad is built—Back to Cheyenne.

ON THE DIVIDE OF THE ATLANTIC AND PACIFIC OCEANS, }
August, 1868. }

TO-DAY the Pacific Railroad climbs over the line
that separates the waters of the oceans. We sit
astride the crest of the continental mountains, and
see the last rail on the Atlantic slope and the first
on the Pacific fastened down. It is an era in our
lives,—it is an era in our national life. Three years
ago, the Pacific Railroad was hardly commenced,—
not a rail was laid this side of the Missouri River;
now there are eight hundred miles of iron track

from that river west; on the other side from the
Pacific Ocean east, six hundred miles are laid; and
early in 1869,—while you are reading these pages,
my friend,—the Continent will be spanned, and the
cars will run from ocean to ocean.   Only the energy
of a Republic could perform such a work in so brief
a time.

Three summers ago, our little party of four persons were ten days and nights in stages in reaching
this point from the Missouri River; now our larger
party of a dozen have been swept up hither in a
day and a half from Omaha, and two days and a
half from Chicago.   Another year the journey from
Boston to San Francisco, that then occupied a full
month, will be compassed in a single week.   Dividing the across-the-continent trip into thirds, this
crest of the mountains is two-thirds the way from
the Atlantic to the Pacific.   Chicago is twelve
hundred miles from Boston; here we are twelve
hundred miles from Chicago; and about the same
distance from San Francisco in the other direction.

Our summer vacation party to these central
mountains of our New West is the outgrowth of
the excursion that Speaker Colfax led across the
Continent in 1865.   Now as then he is the central
figure.   Governor Bross of Illinois comes next, now
as then the favorite of the crowds that gather at
every stopping place for a speech, and the leader in
all our enjoyments.   We miss one of the original
four; but new recruits and the ladies, then denied
us, carry up our numbers to near a dozen.   Chicago
is the gathering-point; there the Old West culmi-

nates, and the New West begins.   Soon she must
cast her lot with the East,—for westward, indeed,
the star of empire takes its way ; but for the season, she sits in the center of railway commerce,
East and West, and, motherly and queenly both,
broods benignantly over the Continent.

Whether you come west to Chicago by Erie or
New York Central, by Pittsburg and Fort Wayne,
by Michigan Southern or Michigan Central, leaving
at the same hour, you are swept into Chicago at
the very same moment.   The thousand mile journey is run on either route to one schedule of time.
Passengers, who part at the supper table at Roches-
ter, bow to each other out of the rival car windows
twenty-four hours later at the junction of the two
Michigan roads in the outer suburbs of Chicago ;
while those, who bade each other good-bye in New
York twelve hours earlier, race along side by side
on the Fort Wayne and Michigan Southern roads,
through the slaughter-house and bone-boiling ad-
jacencies of the great city of the North-west, to
their neighboring station-houses.

It seems strange that in this new and rough
West of ours, where the fight is fresh with all the
elements of nature, and ease and luxury, if not de-
spised, at least are generally postponed, there should
be more comfortable and luxurious accommodations
for railway travel than anywhere else in the world.
Yet it is so.   Europe and the Atlantic states provide on none of their railways as yet so elegant and
ease-giving 'carriages as the saloon and sleeping
and refreshment cars that are offered to travelers

on the long routes of the West. They are the invention of Mr. George W. Pullman, who has thus associated his name forever with one of the greatest improvements in railway travel. Some are provided with kitchen and larder, and will furnish at any hour a meal that rivals Delmonico; and the traveler can leisurely eat breakfast or dinner from his own little private table, as the train sweeps along at the rate of twenty or thirty miles an hour. Their broad, luxurious seats or sofas by day are turned at night into generous beds with clean linen and close curtains if you would have them. The ventilation is perfect; the freedom from dust and cinders only tolerably so; but the chief limitation is in the way of toilette accommodations. One disposed to abandon himself or herself to privacy and much water in this respect chafes somewhat at the common corner and wash-bowl and single looking-glass, however elegant and cleanly; but when a dozen to forty people undertake to keep house for three days or a week in a single car, there must be some sacrifices of fastidiousness to the spirit of travel. That the Pullman car demands so few is the wonder.

These cars are owned by companies distinct from the railroads, and added to the trains of the latter by special arrangements. Additional charges are made to passengers who occupy them, varying with the amount of room and service taken, but about on a par with the prices of first-class hotels for lodgings and meals. To enjoy their comforts to the full, a party of a dozen or twenty should charter the ex-

clusive use of one ; and when the continental pleasure travel to the Pacific sets in next year, this will
be a very common fashion.   Starting from Boston,
New York, Niagara, or Chicago, in your Pullman
parlor, dining-room and bed-room, with servants
to attend to all wants, the journey to San Francisco
may be made with a degree of comfort and luxury,
unequalled heretofore in all the dreams of travel,
and without necessarily leaving the car from the
beginning to the end of the three thousand mile
ride.   Such a company and such a car were ours
from Chicago to the present end of the Railroad and
back, and four days of more comfortable and en-
joyable travel—while half a continent of plain and
mountain and river was unrolled before us—can
hardly be imagined.   A little house organ was
built into the side of our car, and by its aid we
kept time to the music of nature as we rolled over
the prairie and up the hills to the crest of the continental mountains.

From Chicago to Omaha, where is the beginning
of the Pacific Railroad proper, is five hundred
miles, across Northern Illinois and through Central
Iowa, by the Chicago and North-western· Railway,
and crossing the Mississippi River midway.   Two
more roads, lower down in Illinois and Iowa, will be
done next year—those by Rock Island and Burling-
ton—and give Chicago and Omaha three connecting
lines, and all nearly direct.   St. Louis, also, has a
railroad connection with Omaha by the road down
the Missouri River to St. Joseph and Kansas City,
meeting at both points lines across Missouri to its

commercial city.   In fact, this puts Omaha and the
Pacific Road one hundred and twenty-five miles
nearer to St. Louis than to Chicago; but Chicago
is more than that farther east.

Though but a new country, for most of our way,
from Chicago to Omaha, we were rarely out of sight
of the golden stubble of wheat or the rich green
of waving cornfields. The wonder is constant alike
at the richness of the soil, the beauty of the rolling
prairie, the abundance of the harvests, the rapid
settlement and cultivation of the country,—where
all the people came from, and where all the grain
and hay they grow goes to.

Council Bluffs in Iowa and Omaha in Nebraska
are one in inspiration and growth ; but the muddy
Missouri rolls between, and makes them nominal
rivals.   Both are having a rapid development, and
must be great towns.   The roads from the North,
South and East, to connect with the Pacific Road,
must all center at Council Bluffs.   The wide
meadow—three to five miles wide—between the
bluffs and the river will be intersected with their
tracks, and thickly planted with their depots, and
peopled with their dependents.   Three roads—
north to Sioux City, south to St. Joseph and St.
Louis, east to Chicago—are already here ; two
more will come next year ; and in ten years as
many lines will center at this point.   Already
Council Bluffs has eight thousand inhabitants, and
she added thirteen hundred buildings last year.
The older and more attractive parts of the town
lie back on the bluffs and in the wooded ravines

among them—a winning location, where healthfulness and beauty appear combined, and where will gather the real resident population of Council Bluffs.

Omaha rises more directly and symmetrically from the opposite bank; its bluffs or plateaus sweep up sharply from the water, and circle around in a grand amphitheatrical form,—somewhat as Springfield lies to the Connecticut River; you see its majesty of location and its wide-spreading improvements at a glance; the operations of the Pacific Road, of which it is the beginning and the headquarters, have given it almost feverish development; and it already holds a population of fifteen thousand to seventeen thousand. But with such rich conjunction of water and railway communication; with the river at its feet, navigable to the Rocky Mountains, north and west, and to the Gulf of Mexico, south—two thousand miles in either direction; with the workshops and head-quarters of the great Railroad of the Continent within its territory, and all the lines from the East and North and South centering before and around it, to make their connections and transhipments; with a State back of it certainly as large and as rich in agricultural wealth as any in the great West,—Omaha surely need feel no misgiving as to the future, but may proudly accept her destiny as one of the great interior cities of the nation. Directly, a bridge will be raised over the river to Council Bluffs, and then passengers and merchandise can go back and forth in the same cars that they came in from New York or Sacramento.

Now out upon the grand continental Railroad
into the ocean of the Plains. It is five hundred
miles to the base of the central mountains ; up an
imperceptible but steadily.ascending grade of ten
feet to the mile ; and for nearly the whole distance
along by the wide but shallow, fierce but fallow
Platte River, which, gathering in the melted snows
of all this slope of the Rocky Mountains, sweeps
across the wide plains,—that, one day, by dams and
ditches, it is destined to fertilize for miles on each
side and make its wilderness to blossom as the
rose,—and carries the grand tide into the Missouri
below Omaha. For two hundred miles, Nebraska
is slashed by cross rivers, tributaries of Platte or
Missouri ; the land lies in long, beautiful rolls ;
timber is in tolerably good supply ; and the soil is
as fertile as any in the West. The climate is well-
balanced ; oats, corn and wheat yield as richly and
as of fine quality as in any state in the Union ;
and the rapid growth and great wealth of Nebraska
are the surest things in our future. Hardly any
state in the Mississippi and Missouri valleys has
larger capacities. The settlement of her first two
hundred miles west from the Missouri is surpris-
ingly rapid ; well-cultivated farms are rarely out of
sight ; and the population has certainly trebled in
this three years' interval of our visits.

This limit passed, the prairie roll ceases ; timber
and side-streams are no more seen ; the dead level
of the Plains fills the eye ; relieved only, twenty
to thirty miles north and south, by the faint line of
low bluffs, and a scant, irregular growth of cotton-

woods along the line of the Platte itself. But the
grass is strong and green; the soil laughs at the
old nickname of the great American desert; here,
at least, is pasturage unbounded,—wheat, too, I believe, without irrigation, and with irrigation everything. But the first results of the Railroad are to
kill what settlement and cultivation these plains had
reached under the patronage of slow-moving em-
igration, stage-travel, and prairie-schooner freight-
age. The ranches which these supported are now
deserted; the rails carry everybody and everything;
the old roads are substantially abandoned; the old
settlers, losing all their improvements and opportunities, gather in at the railway stations, or move
backwards or forwards to greater local developments. They are the victims, in turn, of a higher
civilization; they drove out the Indian, the wolf,
and the buffalo; the locomotive whistles their occupation away; and invites back for the time the
original occupants.

The day's ride grows monotonous. The road is
as straight as an arrow. Every dozen or fifteen
miles is a station,—two or three sheds and a water-
spout and woodpile; every one hundred miles or
so a home or division depot, with shops, eating-
house, "saloons" uncounted, a store or two, a few
cultivated acres, and the invariable half a dozen
seedy, staring loafers, that are a sort of fungi in-
digenous to American railways. The meals are
abundant and good,—breakfast, dinner and supper
each the same as the other, and only apt to be uncertain in bread and butter. We yawn over the un-

changing landscape and the unvarying model of the
stations, and lounge and read by day, and go to bed
early at night. But the clear, dry air charms; the
half dozen soldiers hurriedly marshalled into line
at each station as the train comes up, suggest the
Indians; we catch a glimpse of antelopes in the
distance; and we watch the holes of the prairie
dogs for their piquant little owners and their traditional companions of owls and snakes,—but never
see the snakes.

Fremont (46 miles from Omaha) and Columbus
(91) are the most considerable and promising settlements of Nebraska on the line of the road. The
latter disputed the political capital with Omaha, but
Lincoln, little more than a paper town as yet, and off
the railway line, has won it from both. ˉOld Fort
Kearney, 200 miles out, a representative of the old-
time life of the Plains, is fading away. The chief
stations of the Railroad, so far, are Grand Island (153
miles), North Platte (291), Sidney (414), Cheyenne
(516), and Laramie (572). Julesburg, last year so
lively a settlement, and at one time before an important military post, is now abandoned altogether,—a
few log and board shanties and turf huts are all that
remain of its former high uncivilization. Cheyenne
alone takes on the air of permanency and feels the
hopes of promise. After " Hell," as the end town
of the Railroad has been appropriately called, moved
on, it was a serious question with her whether to be
or not to be,—whether she was anything or nothing. The problem seems to be solved in her favor.
She stands at the end of the Plains, at the begin-

ning of the Mountains; the Railroad must have important shops here; it is the point of divergence
for Colorado to the South, and the Railroad to Denver connects with the main line here,—ultimately
the Kansas or St. Louis Pacific Railroad will, as
Congress has ordered, make its connection by this
branch; a fine agricultural country surrounds, feeding the mountains beyond,—altogether material
enough to make a permanency of Cheyenne. She
has now three or four thousand inhabitants, who
are settling down into reasonable soberness and
serious work; three daily papers struggle for support; several good church buildings are erected or
erecting; brick and stone are supplanting canvass
and rough boards as building materials; and taverns
and restaurants and stores well respond to all human appetites and needs and tastes. Though the
town is six thousand feet above the level of the sea,
it lies on an open prairie country, and the mountains are only dimly discernible in the distance.   It
is the principal settlement of the new territory of
Wyoming, but so near Colorado, that the latter
territory covets and half claims it.

Now the road grows more interesting. We do
not enter mountains, except in fancy,—they have
been levelled for our track; but the plain ascends
rapidly; the debris of the old mountains stand
around in fantastic shapes; the forms of the remaining mountains rise vast and majestic, blue and white
and black, in the far distance, north and south; in
thirty-two miles the track ascends over two thousand feet, but so uniformly is the rise distributed

that at no point is the grade above eighty feet to
the mile; and at Sherman or Evans's Pass, we are
eight thousand two hundred and sixty-two feet
above the sea level—the highest point in the whole
line. of the Pacific Railroad, yet the crest, not of
the. main or continental range of mountains, but
of its eastern line of "Black Hills," so called. Out
of narrower plain, free from these ruins of the old
mountains, down a thousand feet or so, the road
next enters upon and crosses the wide Laramie
Plains; a trifle sheltered, yet open to sharp suns
and long, piercing breezes, and selected for their various attractions for the summer homes of the railroad officials. These were famous hunting-grounds
of the Indians; agreeable resting-places for the
emigrant caravans of old; and long the chief outpost of the army in the mountain region.

All this section of the road for one hundred and
fifty miles west of Cheyenne possesses the greatest
novelty and charm for the traveler. The senses all
dilate with what is spread before and around him;
rich black mountains bound the horizon north and
south; a dash of snow on peak or side occasionally
enlivens the view and deepens the coloring; along
your pathway are fine valleys or broader plains,·
rich in grass and flowers; nature has fashioned it
for a railroad; scattered around in valley or plain,
as the track approaches the summit, are monuments of rock, grotesquely or symmetrically ar-
ranged; here a wall as if for a bulwark, there the
ruin of cathedral or fort, again a half-finished building, anon the fashion of a huge, dismasted screw

steamer, with paddle astern and pilot-boat ahead; over all an atmosphere so pure that the eye seems to take in all space, and so dry and exhilarating that life titillates at every avenue, and we mount as if on angel's wings. Here would seem to be the fountain of health; and among these hills and plains is surely to be many a summer resort for the invalid and the pleasure-seeker in the by no means distant future. The hills have timber, though the plains are bare of it, and the water runs pure and bright, and carries trout in abundance, as plains and mountains give deer, mountain sheep, antelope and grouse. This whole wide pathway up and over the mountains seems to have been fashioning for its present use for ages. The hills have wasted into plain; those solid walls of feldspar and granite disintegrated and dissipated into a fine gravel, that is the very perfection of a railway bed; while these "buttes" or monuments of remaining rock, that lie scattered about with such picturesque effect, are all that are left, the very kernel, so to speak, of what was once but a close succession of real rocky mountains—a Pelion upon Ossa that forbade passage to wheel of wagon or car.

But the next section of one hundred and fifty miles is a sad contrast. The charms of atmosphere and of distant mountains remain; but the green grass, the flowers, the pure water, the oases of trees, all depart, and we have a dreary waste of sage bush, a barren, alkali, dusty soil, little water, and that bitter and poisonous. This is the Bitter Creek country, so horrible to slow emigrant travel, so

painful to stage passengers. The eye has no joy,
the lips no comfort through it; the sun burns by
day, the cold chills at night; the fine, impalpable,
poisonous dust chokes and chafes and chaps you
everywhere. It is within this region that my letter
is dated, and that the track crosses the continental
divide. Rolling hills abound, but no mountains.
The track winds easily along; but a water train
has to be added to the usual supply trains, and the
expense of construction is greatly increased by
the distance which all material and all food and
drink have to be drawn. Deep wells will in the
future relieve the poverty and poisonousness of
the surface water, whose alkali elements not only
render it unfit for drink but impossible of use in
the boilers of the engines.

Spite of the obstacles, however, the track marches
on with magic rapidity. Ten to fifteen thousand
men are at work on the grading of the three hundred miles between this point and Salt Lake valley.
Following the completion of their work come the
gangs of track-layers with their supply trains. First
the ties or sleepers, brought up from below or out
of the neighboring hills, and carried several miles
ahead of the train by innumerable mule teams.
Then rails and spikes are transferred to platform
cars and pushed up to the end of the track; and
by help of horse and a dozen practiced men, working like automatons with brains, the iron lengths
are dropped in place, spiked down, the car rolled
over them, the work repeated, and again and again,
at the rate of from *three* to *eight* miles a day,—the

only limit yet found being the power of the completed road to bring up sleepers and rails to the supply trains of the contractors. The gangs of track-layers number in all from four hundred to five hundred; are picked men; live on the train or in tents which the train brings along as the track progresses; and are fed by the contractors in so good a style that no apologies were necessary in inviting our party of ladies and gentlemen to dine with them, and no hesitation felt on our part in accepting, nor any repentance at having accepted. It was one of the "squarest" meals of our whole trip so far.

For a few weeks now, Benton, in this Bitter Creek country, is the end of the open road, and here passengers and freight going west are transhipped, and here are temporarily gathered that motley crew of desperadoes, outcasts and reckless speculators, that are following the road's progress, and rioting in the license and coarseness of unorganized society. It is a most aggravated specimen of the border town of America, not inaptly called "Hell on Wheels," and unknown to all other civilizations or barbarisms. One to two thousand men, and a dozen or two women, are camped on the alkali plain in tents and board shanties; not a tree, not a shrub, not a blade of grass visible; the dust ankle deep as you walk through it, and so fine and volatile that the slightest breeze loads the air with it, irritating every sense and poisoning half of them; a village of a few variety stores and shops, and many restaurants and grog-shops; by day disgusting, by night dangerous;

almost everybody dirty, most filthy, and with the marks of lowest vice ; averaging a murder a day ; gambling and drinking, hurdy-gurdy dancing and the vilest of sexual commerce, the chief business and pastime of the hours,—this is Benton. Like its predecessors on the track, it fairly festers in corruption, disorder and death, and would rot, even in this dry air, should it outlast a brief sixty-day life. In a few weeks, its tents will be struck, its shanties razed, and with their dwellers will move on fifty or a hundred miles farther to repeat their life for another brief day. Where these people came from originally; where they will go to when the road is finished, and their occupation is over, are both puzzles too intricate for me. Hell would appear to have been raked to furnish them ; and to it they will naturally return after graduating here, fitted for its highest seats and its most diabolical service.

Beyond this one hundred and fifty mile section of desert country, that marks the divide between the waters of the two oceans, the road crosses Green River and enters upon the descent into the Salt Lake basin. The country here changes rapidly; it is broken by mountain ranges, and coursed by fresh rivers ; and every way becomes most interesting to the traveler, and most difficult for the railroad constructor. The section from Green River to the Salt Lake valley is the hardest part of the whole line of the Union Pacific Road to build; heavy rock cuttings and embankments, sharp curves, and tunnels are necessitated ; yet there is nothing in it all so serious and expensive as the

work on the line of the railroads through and over
the Alleghany Mountains, or worse than that the
Boston and Albany Railroad encountered west of
Springfield.   The traveler will find pleasure, however, where the contractors met labor; the wonderful Church Butte, the charming high valley region
about Fort Bridger, the narrow, rock-embraced
canyons or gorges of Echo and Weber, the white-
capped Wasatch Mountains,—all will awaken his
enthusiasm and wonder, and lead him down to the
settlements and civilization of the Mormon saints
in a frame of pleasurable and curious excitement.
He will need all its stimulus, however, to carry him
contented over the new and wider desert country
that the road will yet take him, along and beyond
the Humboldt valley, through northern Nevada,
and on to the now double-welcome glories of the
Sierra Nevadas.   And here upon the threshold of
California, we leave him to find his own way.

Everybody inquires how the Pacific Railroad is
built?   Well or ill—as faithful as fast—befitting or
betraying the royal endowment of the American
people?   A monosyllable will not answer the question.   Well, with a qualification ; ill, with a qualification.   As well, certainly, as new roads are generally built in America—better surely than the
North-western Road is built across Iowa.   As well,
too, as is consistent with such speed.   The ties are
plenty, a third thicker at least than is usual in the
East; the rails as good as the Pennsylvania iron
consciences and poverty will permit ; and the ad-
justments all faithfully made and by competent

workmen. I could wish the bed had been thrown
up a foot higher across the Plains, to escape the
flood of possible heavy rains and the drift of snows;
long sections are certainly imperfectly ballasted, or
not at all; wooden bridges and culverts need to be
rebuilt with stone; tressle-work should be replaced
by embankments; and embankments need widening; many curves and circles should be cut across,
the line straightened and shortened; and grades
lowered or evened up. But the builders agree as
to all this, except perhaps the hight of the bed
across the Plains, and are proceeding with the improvements and reconstructions as fast as the
greater necessity for pushing on to the end will
permit them. The only dispute there can be is as
to the degree or extent which these completions and
reconstructions are necessary or should be required.

The road has been and will be such a mine of
wealth to its owners, they should be held by public
and government to a strict performance of all their
obligations,—they should give us in return for our
gifts of money and land and privilege a thoroughly
first-class road in every respect. But, on the other
hand, exacting security for the perfection, they
should be allowed generous time to do it in. The
materials, stone, ballasting and timber, for all the
work required, are upon the line; and when the rush
of progress is over, and the road opened through,
then the work of bringing up every part and
every detail to perfection should be insisted upon
by the one party, and cheerfully executed by the
other. Self-interest invites the managers to this

fidelity; they have found the road most profitable to build; they are likely to find it as profitable to own and run; and dependent as they must largely be upon the favor of public opinion and the protection and care of the government, aside from the necessity of having the road in thorough condition for its safe and profitable use, they will see how desirable it is they should leave no cause for complaint in the condition and management of the property.

No internal improvement was ever so generously endowed,—none was ever so wonderfully built. The government bounty was voted in ignorance of the difficulties and cost of the work. They have proven much less than was expected. The entire road from the Missouri River to the Pacific Ocean is about one thousand seven hundred miles long. The California company builds six hundred miles, the New York company about one thousand one hundred, and their junction is near Salt Lake. Congress voted sixteen thousand dollars government bonds per mile of plain country; thirty-two thousand dollars per mile of more difficult territory; and forty-eight thousand dollars per mile of the higher and rougher mountains passed over; and it also authorized the companies to issue mortgage bonds of their own to equal amounts, which should take precedence in security of the government bonds. From one-half to two-thirds of the entire line is probably through "plain" country, yet, from a mixture of deception and ignorance, only about one-third was so counted. The average govern-

ment grant was thirty thousand dollars a mile, and
the companies' first bonds, which have found ready
sale, just doubled this sum as the cash provision for
the construction of the road, or sixty thousand dollars per mile.   But the actual cost has not probably
been over half this, or not far in excess of the government grant alone,—certainly, with equipment,
it will not average over forty thousand dollars per
mile.   This would leave a net cash profit on the
building and opening of the road of thirty-four
millions dollars.   But, back of all this, the companies have the capital stock of the road, and own
half the lands for a width of twenty miles along
their tracks.   There never was such a gigantic
speculation on the American continent at least;
and it is safe to predict that no other railroad will
ever win such largess from the government as this
has.

To snow how deceived or mistaken the government agents were in the character of the work to
be done, the traveler only need to look at the one
hundred and fifty miles of road west from Cheyenne, and remember that this is the section for
which they allowed the highest price of forty-eight
thousand dollars a mile as heavy mountain work.
In fact, it is about as fine a country to build a
railroad through as lies on the face of the globe.
It is one long, inclined plane, with a fine, disintegrated granite for its soil, worked by plow and
scraper, and affording the solidest and most permanent road bed that exists in America.   Only a
few hills had to be cut through, or embankments

made, or streams crossed.   The California company had no such rich streak of luck as this; their forty-eight thousand dollars a mile section was grievously heavy mountain work, over the rough and broken Sierra Nevadas, requiring heavy rock cuttings and many tunnels.   But they had, to make up for it, no "plain" or sixteen thousand dollars a mile track at all; it was all forty-eight thousand dollars and thirty-two thousand dollars a mile, while many of their miles were as easy to build as the line across the Plains of the eastern section.

But no matter now!   Only by such appeal to cupidity have we got this continental roadway opened so soon,—a gift to our nationality, to our commerce, to our wealth, that is worth in five years more than it all cost.   And now if the gigantic corporations that own and use it will but let our politics alone, give the country faithful service and at a fair price, and spend some of their profits in opening branch lines to Montana, Idaho, and Oregon, we will gladly give them welcome to their fortunes, and cry quits.

The path and the profits of the Pacific Railroad are likely to be for some time fresh subjects in our American lives, and so justify this long letter about them.   We turn back the track to Cheyenne, and thence follow the mountains down to Denver to begin our real Summer Vacation in Colorado.

II.

TO DENVER AND THERE.

Where the Mountains Lie—The Stage Ride from Cheyenne to
Denver—Scenes in the Stage-Coach at Night—Meals on the
Road—How Denver Looks—Its Growth, Attainments, and
Prospects—The Mountain View from the Town—Denver and
Salt Lake City Rivals in Beauty of Location and Attraction for
Travelers.

· DENVER, Colorado, August, 1868.

IT is the old story over again—the railroads do
not show you the best of the country. Their tracks
run through the back yards in towns, and away
from the hills and among the barren wastes of the
interior. You no more see the Rocky Mountains
in riding over the Pacific Railroad than you do New
York in going through the Fourth Avenue tunnels,
or Springfield in steaming by the mechanic shops
and restaurants of Railroad Row. Nature graded
a grand pathway for the locomotive across our Continent; the mountains fall back to the right of us and
to the left of us,—so far away that we catch only the
dim outline of their greatness,—leaving but here
and there a quaint ruin of or majestic monument
to her mighty labor, that civilization may go by
steam from ocean to ocean. The great mountain
center of the Continent lies below the present rail-

road line; it looms up in the distance at Cheyenne;
it marches along the southern horizon as you sweep
up and across the magnificent Laramie Plains; it
cheers you through the rolling alkali dust of the
Bitter Creek country; and it shoots its spurs in
beauty and in power before you, as you seek, more
slowly, a descending path into the Salt Lake basin.
But would you behold it in all its majestic grandeur,
its multiplied folds of hight, with fields of ice and
snow and rock, its beauty of infinite form and color;
its wealth of flora and its wealth of gold and silver,
—all the grand landscape and the hidden promise
of the finest mountain region that the world holds,—
then you must switch off from the main road, and
come into the heart of Colorado, which is the very
heart of our western Continent.

Bear in mind, too, that the great Pacific Railroad
does not touch Colorado. It goes a few miles
above the northern border. A branch road is now
building from the main track at Cheyenne down to
Denver, the capital and focal point of the state.
While waiting for that to be finished, next year, we
travel this one hundred miles in a six-horse coach.
If we could do it all by daylight, nothing could be
more pleasant. The road lies across the last fifty
miles of the Plains,—through high rolling green
prairies, cut every fifteen or twenty miles by a
vigorous river, with border of rich and cultivated
intervale, and line of trees marking its progress from
mountain debouch to the slow-sinking, wide-reach-
ing horizon,—to the right the grim mountains with
towering tops of rock and snow,—to the left the un-

ending prairie ocean, with only an occasional cabin
and scattered herd of cattle to break its majestic
solitude and indicate human settlement; there is
such magnificent out-doorness in the continuous
scene as no narrower or differently combined landscape can offer, and so long as the day lasts it is a
thing of beauty and of joy.   But it is a twenty hours'
ride, and the stage arrangements make a night of it.
And in stage-riding it is peculiarly true that it is the
first night that costs.   It is more intolerable than the
combination of the succeeding half-dozen, were the
journey prolonged for a week; the breaking-in is
fearful,—the prolongation is bearable.   The air gets
cold, the road grows dusty and chokes, or rough and
alarms you; the legs become stiff and numb, the
temper edges; everybody is overcome with sleep,
but can't stay asleep,—the struggle of contending
nature racks every nerve, fires every feeling; everybody flounders and knocks about against everybody
else in helpless despair; perhaps the biggest man
in the stage will really get asleep, which doing
he involuntarily and with irresistible momentum
spreads himself, legs, boots, arms and head, over
the whole inside of the coach; the girls screech,
the profane swear; some lady wants a smelling
bottle out of her bag and her bag is somewhere on
the floor,—nobody knows where,—but found it must
be; everybody's back hair comes down, and what
is nature and what is art in costume and character
is revealed,—and then, hardest trial of all, morning
breaks upon the scene and the feelings,—everybody
dirty, grimy, faint, "all to pieces," cross,—such a

disenchanting exhibition! The girl that is lovely then, the man who is gallant and serene,—let them be catalogued for posterity, and translated at once,—heaven cannot spare such ornaments; and they are too aggravating for earth.

Every ten miles we stop to change horses, and the driver, night or day, signalizes the approach to a station by a miniature war-whoop, that, as the Bostonians say of their great organ, "must be heard to be appreciated,"—it is certainly rather startling to new ears. Every thirty miles or so, a "home" station and a "square meal." Dinner, supper and breakfast are all alike, and invariably generous and good, more uniformly so, indeed, than those along the railroad line from Chicago to the mountains. We missed willingly some of one sort of "home" stations, that we encountered out here three years ago in the "Across the Continent" ride,—single-roomed turf cabins, bare dirt floors, milkless coffee, rancid bacon, stale beans, and green bread, and "if you don't like these, help yourself to mustard;" but we welcomed heartily, at the Laporte station, where is the most of a village on the road, our old host and hostess, with whom the Indians then prevailed on us, in their charming fashion, to pass a sweet and silent Sunday in their little retreat of Virginia Dale park in the mountains on the old road,—lady and gentleman now as then by diviner gifts than those of milliner or tailor. It was pleasant to see they had prospered, and got out among neighbors, where Indian raids, of which they had survived no fewer than eight in their solitary Dale

station, now abandoned, were less threatening;
pleasant to have the ladies confirm the picture in
"Across the Continent" on comparison with the
original; pleasantest of all, perhaps, to find *she* had
not forgotten our weakness for good victual. Those
sup well who sup with our heroine of Virginia Dale,
and if they would have especial grace and greeting,
let them prove acquaintance with the "Colfax party."

The Vice-President often dwells on "the two
kinds of welcome," and it was the other kind that
we met at the next eating-place. Our stage was
an "extra," and "ran wild," and so came along un-
awares. It was a trifle rough, therefore, to rouse a
lone woman, at one o'clock in the night, to get us
some supper or breakfast,—whichever you choose
to call it. She could do it, she said, but she didn't
quite like to. But who could resist the gallant Vice-
President, whether pleading for ballot or breakfast;
or the offers of help from the ladies; or the final
suggestion of the driver? She wavered at the first;
the second operated as a challenge to her capacity;
and the third was irresistible. There is no king on
his route like a stage driver,—he has a "dreadful
winning way" with him, both for horses and women.
The philosophy of it I do not understand, but the
fact is universal and stubborn; he is the successful
diplomat of the road; no meal can be begun till he
is in place; and there are no vacant seats where he
drives,—even the cold night air would not send our
girls off his box, and inside, during this long ride.
So, at two o'clock in the morning, we sat down to
beef and ham and potatoes, tea and coffee, bread

and butter, pies, cakes and canned fruits,—not even the edges of the "squareness" of the meal rubbed off, and good humor everywhere.

We cross the rivers Cache-a-la Poudre,—which indicates that some Frenchman deposited his powder here aforetime,—St. Vrains, Big Thompson, Little Thompson, Boulder, Clear Creek, and finally the South Platte, to which all the others are tributary; and, having left Cheyenne at ten o'clock in the forenoon, gay and aggressive, we are tumbled out of the stage at Denver at eight the next morning, feeble and flabby, hungry and humble, with a dreadful "morning after" feeling and appearance and movement about us.

But the air of Denver, both inside and outside the houses, is very recuperating; we were soon toned up, and began to look about us. The town has spread out and settled down a good deal within three years. Things look less brisk, but more substantial and assured. The town "feels its oats" less and its dignity more. It has passed its hot and fickle days, when gamblers reigned, and "to be or not to be" was the everlasting question that fretted everybody who owned real estate, and with which they, in a sort of your-money-or-your-life manner, assaulted every stranger the moment he got out of the stage. Now, though trade is dull, and I have seen but one fight since I came to town, the Denverites all wear a fixed fact sort of air, and most of them are able to tell you, in a low and confidential chuckle, calling for envy rather than sympathy, that they own a quarter section just out there on the bluff, to which the town is rapidly spreading, and where the capitol buildings and the fine residences will all be located, or a few corner lots down near the river, where the mills and the factories are destined to rise in the near future.   Long lines of brick stores already give permanent and prosperous air to the town; its dry and its wet rivers are both newly bridged; irrigating ditches scatter water freely through streets, lawns and gardens, and now flowers and fruits, trees and vegetables lend their civilizing influences and their permanent attractions to the place; national banks emit their greenbacks and will "do" your little note most graciously at from one to two per cent a month and "a grab mortgage" behind it; Episcopal Bishop Randall from Boston has established an excellent school for girls; the Catholics have a larger educational establishment; the Methodists have the handsomest church and wear the best clothes; the Baptists and Congregationalists are lively and aggressive; the stores are closed Sundays; the nights are quiet and the police have a sinecure; free schools are organized; and three daily papers and two independent weeklies are published in the town.   Kitchen girls are scarce and a dear luxury, with pay at fifty dollars to seventy-five dollars a month; but the consequence is that the cooking is excellent, and people live "first rate."   The dwelling-houses are mostly small, a single story or a story and a half, but within are comforts and luxuries in abundance, and one house boasts a true Van Dyke. The emigrant and the traveler must "move on" by

Denver if he would get beyond the organization of the best American social and intellectual life.

I see I have spoken of Denver's "dry river," which calls for a parenthetical paragraph in explanation. The South Platte sweeps around the lower part of the town, broad and turbulent, of certain volume but uncertain track, useless for navigation but excellent for irrigation; but more sharply through the center of the business section lies Cherry Creek, now a broad bottom of dry sand, and only occasionally enlivened with any water. For years after the founding of the town, none appeared in its bed, and supposing it to have been deserted altogether, the people builded and lived in the bottom. Stores, shops and dwellings, streets and blocks appeared there; it was the heart of the town; the printing office was there, also the city records; but of a sudden, after a heavy rain, there came a flood pouring down the old river bed, not gradually and in rivulets, to warn, but a full-blown stream marched abreast with torrent force and almost lightning speed, reclaimed its own, and swept everything that had usurped its place into destruction. Since then, the people have paid respect to Cherry Creek; at some seasons of the year there is still a little water in its sands, but for the most part it is dry through the town; but nobody builds in the bed, and bridges over its path pay tribute to what it has been and may be again. Farther up its line, there is water in it now; but the sands consume and an irrigating ditch seduces it all away before it reaches the limits of the city.

Her central location, under the mountains, in the Plains section of the state, gives Denver a fine climate the year through ; is favorable for trade to all parts of the state ; secures to her the outgo and the income of the mining districts ; makes her also the · chief market for all the productions of the farming counties, and the focal point for all travel to and from the mountains, as well as north to the Railroad, and south to New Mexico ; and endows her with a scene of mountain panoramic beauty, one hundred miles long, now touched with clouds, now radiant with sunshine, then dark with rocks and trees, again white with snow, now cold, now warm, but always inspiring in grandeur, and ever unmatched by the possession of any other city of Europe or America. The finest views of these mountains are obtained farther out in the Plains, where the more distant peaks come into sight, and the depth and variety, as well as the hight and beauty of the range, are realized ; and wider and older travelers than I,—who have seen the Cordilleras of South America from the sea, as well the Alps from Berne,—join in the judgment that no grand mountain view exists, that surpasses this, as seen from the high roll of the prairie just out of Denver, and over which the town is fast spreading, and so on from twenty to forty miles farther east.   The one point of grandest view is located at the last "home station" on the Smoky Hill road, about thirty-five miles east from Denver, and along which the St. Louis Pacific Road will probably be built another year.

With these charms of climate and landscape, with

a settled and intelligent and prosperous population already of four thousand to five thousand, with business connections and facilities, social order and attractions, religious and educational institutions, all well organized, and fed by their own interior force,— growing from within out, and not simply by fresh importations of eastern material,—and holding the conceded position of the social, political and commercial capital of the state, Denver has a gratifying future of growth before it. Another year will bring through it the Pacific Railroad on the St. Louis route, connecting here with the branch of the main or central road that drops down from Cheyenne; a railroad is already commenced, also, towards the mining centers of the mountains by the Clear Creek valley; and it cannot be long before a southern road will be demanded, down from Denver along the base of the Mountains to southern Colorado and Santa Fe. Not unlikely, indeed, it will prove wiser to carry the first southern Pacific Railroad around this way, rather than to strike diagonally across to Santa Fe from the present terminus of the St. Louis Road, as is proposed, for this route is through a rich and already partly developed agricultural country, while that goes by half or wholly barren table-lands, not likely to be at all occupied for many years, and never capable like this of holding a large population.

Coal and iron and clay are found in the neighborhood; the hills give timber; the valleys every grain and vegetable and many fruits; and Denver cannot well escape a steady and healthy growth, and the destiny of becoming one of the most per-

manently prosperous, as it will be certainly one of
the most beautiful of our great western interior
cities.   I rank it along with Salt Lake City.   Both
are off the main line of the continental railroad;
but both have locations amid developed natural
wealth and conceded natural beauty, that must com-
mand their future, and make it one of power and
prosperity.   Six hundred miles apart, with the continental range of mountains separating them, there
can be no rivalry between them, save in social graces
and pleasure attractions, and here the Mormon supremacy in Salt Lake will give Denver great ad-
vantages.

III.

THE GEOGRAPHY OF COLORADO.

The Back-bone of the Continent—The Mother Mountains of America—The Three Great Divisions of Colorado—Her Plains, Her Folds of High Mountain Ranges, Her Great Natural, Elevated Parks—North, Middle and South Parks; their Surroundings and their Beauties—The Unknown West of Colorado.

IN THE MOUNTAINS, Colorado, August, 1868.

As Pennsylvania is the key-stone in the Atlantic belt or arch of states, so is Colorado the key-stone in the grand continental formation. She holds the back-bone, the stiffening of the Republic. Lying a huge square block in the very center of the vast region bounded by the Mississippi valley on the east, the Pacific Ocean on the west, and British America and Mexico north and south, the continental mountain chain here dwells in finest proportions, exaggerates, puffs itself up and spreads itself around with a perfect wantonness and luxuriance of power,—great fountains of gold and silver, and lead and copper, and zinc and iron,—great fountains of water that pours itself in all directions through the whole interior of the Continent, feeding a wealth of agriculture that is little developed and never yet dreamed of even,—great fountains of

health in pure, dry and stimulating air,—great
fountains of natural beauty; she may proudly bid
the nation come to her for strength, for wealth, for
vigor,—for rest and restoration,—and may well
call her mountains the Sierra Madre, the Mother
Mountains of the Continent.

Her geographical prominence and parentage are
but type and promise of her future relations to
the developed and developing life of the nation.
Stretching two hundred and sixty miles north and
south, and three hundred and seventy-five miles
east and west, her territory has three natural sub-
divisions. The eastern third is of the Plains, and
forms their western section,—a high rolling plateau
from four thousand to five thousand feet above the
sea level, richly watered by streams from the mountains, the strips along the rivers ripe for abundant
harvests of grain and fruits and vegetables, the
whole already the finest pasture land of the Continent, and with irrigation, for which the streams
afford ready facility, capable of most successful
cultivation,—beautiful in its wide, treeless sea of
green and gray, with waves of land to break the
monotony and lift the eye on to the great panorama
of mountains, snow-slashed and snow-capped, that
hangs over its western line through all its length of
two hundred and sixty miles, and marks the second
or middle division of the state. This is of about
equal width,—mountains one hundred, one hundred
and fifty, two hundred miles deep,—on, on to the
west, till even this pure air tires of carrying the eye
over peak on peak, over range on range,—you think

you must look over into Brigham Young's fertile valleys, and trace the Colorado River out of its grand
mystery, even if the outer and faintest rim does not
shadow forth the Sierra Nevada of California.   .

Starting from an elevation at the end of the
Plains of five thousand to five thousand five hundred feet, these mountains rapidly carry you up to
eight thousand, ten thousand, thirteen thousand,
near to fifteen thousand feet above the sea level.
Nine, ten, and twelve thousand feet peaks are scattered everywhere,—they are the mountains,—while
those that mount to thirteen or fourteen thousand
are plenty enough to be familiar, and are indeed
rarely out of sight. They do not form a simple
line, ascending from one and descending to another
plain or valley, but are a dozen lines folded on, and
mingled among each other, in admirable confusion ;
opening to let their superfluous waters flow out ;
closing to hold their treasures and defy the approach of man ; gathering up all their strength, as
it were, to make a peak or two of extra massive
proportions, cold with snow and dreary with rock ;
and shading down into comparatively tender hills,
that woo the forests and the flowers to their very
summits. The line of peaks that divide the waters
that flow to the Atlantic from those coursing into
the Pacific,—"the divide," par excellence,—twists
and turns through the territory, very much in the
style of a long and double-backed bow, making an
almost entire circle sometimes, and then coming
back to its mission as a north and south line.
Within its huge folds are other "divides," sepa-

rating the feeders to rival rivers of the same continental side, or rival feeders of the same river, and
other ranges with peaks as high as the parent
range; and within and among them all, the hills,
as if tired of hight and perpendicularity, give way
to wide plains or prairies, with all the beauties and
characteristics of plains and prairies outside the
mountain region, and the added charm of holding
little baby mountains of their own to diversify the
landscape and feed forest and stream, while up and
around them grow, through woods and grassy openings, the grand parent ranges that guard and en-
fold what are well called NATURAL PARKS.

These Parks are a distinctive and remarkable
feature of this mountain center or belt of Colorado. They open upon the traveler at frequent intervals in charming unexpectedness; rich with grass
and water, with trees and flowers, with soft beauty
of outline and warm beauty of color, in most admirable contrast to the rough rocks and white snow
of the high ranges around. Most of these Parks
are, of course, petite,—little wide valleys around the
heads of single streams, or the conjunctions of several, or the homes of sweet lakes; but there are
four great ones that mark the phenomenon and
give the name. These are North Park, Middle
Park, South Park and San Luis Park, varying in
size from twenty by fifty miles to one hundred by
two hundred, or say from Rhode Island to Massachusetts,—little episodes and interjections among
these mountains, by whose size, as thus stated,
you may take in some sense of the extent and

majesty of the region, of which they are a sub-
feature, as a whole.

The North Park extends up to the northern line
of the territory and within thirty or forty miles of
the Pacific Railroad; through and out of it flow the
head waters of the North Platte; its streams are
thicker with trout, and its sage brush and buffalo
grass and wooded hill-sides offer more deer and
wolves and antelopes and bears than are found in
the lower and more frequented Parks, but its soil is
colder as its elevation is higher, and its charms of
color and vegetation more stinted.   Middle Park
lies next below, and separated by a single but
high sub-range of the main mountains.   This is
fifty miles wide by seventy miles long, and as the
continental divide sweeps around on its eastern
side, all its waters flow into the Colorado of the
West and so into the Pacific.   But it embraces
within itself several high ranges of hills and two
or three different valleys.   The great peaks of the
territory lie marshaled around it,—Long's Peak,
Gray's Peaks, and Mount Lincoln, north-east, south-
east and south-west, each from thirteen thousand to
fourteen thousand five hundred feet high; and snow-
topped mountains circle its whole area.   Milder and
more beautiful in landscape than the North, it yet
falls behind its neighbor on the other side, the
South Park, which is thirty miles wide and sixty
long, and, fellowshiping with the North Park, comes
into the inner tail of the bow, carries the continental
divide on its west, and furnishes the waters of the
Arkansas and the South Platte.

This (the South) is the more beautiful of the
Parks and the better known. Mining discoveries
within and around it have opened roads through it,
and bordered it with settlements. It offers a remarkable combination of the beauties of the Plains
and those of the Mountains. They mingle and mix
in charming association. Wide areas of rich prairie
open out before the level eye ; upraise it or turn
one side, and grand snowy mountains carry the
sight up among the clouds ; and between these
types of natural beauty are plentiful shadings in
gently rolling hills, long level banks, thick and
diversified forests, bright and bountiful streams,—
all the grand panorama of natural beauty that hill
and valley, mountain and plain, winter and summer, snow and verdure, trees and rocks, water and
waste can produce in combination and comparison,
is here spread before the spectator, not from a
single spot or in a single hour of his travel, but
from mile to mile, from day's journey to day's journey, ever the same various scene, yet ever shifting
in its kaleidoscopic alliances and changes.

The San Luis Park lies along and around the
Arkansas and its tributaries in Southern Colorado
and Northern New Mexico, is the largest and perhaps the most varied of the series of great Parks,
centers about a grand lake, and is rich alike in
agricultural and mineral promise. The Indians
have robbed us of our promised peep into its lines,
and we know it only by its kinship to those we
have visited, and the enthusiastic descriptions of
those to whom it is familiar. But the South Park

as yet takes the palm among the Coloradians, perhaps only, however, because it is the more accessible, and its beauties more thoroughly explored. Certainly it lies more closely in the lap of the great mountains ; and Mount Lincoln and Pike's Peak, perhaps the most noted and remarkable of all the high peaks of the territory, sentinel it north and south, feed it from their snows, protect it from the rough winds, shadow it from the sharp suns.

In spite of these great elevations, the traveler carries summer skies as he keeps summer scenes with him at this season in most of his excursions among the mountains and their parks in Colorado. We borrow our ideas of mountain travel and mountain hights from Switzerland and the White Mountains of New Hampshire. Among them both, vegetation ceases at about five thousand feet above the sea level, and perpetual snow reigns among the Alps at seven thousand to eight thousand feet, and would in the White Mountains if they went as high. But here in these vaster mountain regions than either of Western America, the hills themselves only begin to rise from the Plains at an elevation of five thousand five hundred feet. And at that hight, though the nights are always deliciously cool, the summer's days are as warm as, if not warmer than they ever are in the valleys of the New England States, and snow enough for sleighing or to force the cattle to shelter or other food than the prairie grass is only a rare chance,— a memory of the oldest, or a dream of the youngest inhabitant. At six thousand or seven thousand

feet, in the valleys of the mountains, the small
grains and the tenderer vegetables are successfully
cultivated, and at seven thousand five hundred and
eight thousand five hundred feet, potatoes, turnips
and cabbages thrive. The Middle Park ranges
from seven thousand seven hundred to nine thousand feet high in its level sections, and the South
from six thousand five hundred to seven thousand
five hundred, while the higher plains and embraced
hills of both run up to ten thousand and even
eleven thousand feet. Yet grass grows richly and
abundantly through both ; hay is a great natural
crop, and is cured already for all the wants that
can be reached ; and in the lower parts of the
South Park, cattle winter out of doors, and the
smaller grains and hardier vegetables are grown
with great success and profit. Flowers are beautiful and abundant up to ten thousand or eleven
thousand feet,—so beautiful and abundant that I
must reserve them for special description,—the
largest and best timber grows at nine thousand
to eleven thousand feet, and trees do not cease
till you pass above eleven thousand five hundred
feet, while the real, absolute and perpetual snow
line, — such snow and ice as are found univer-
sally in Switzerland at eight thousand feet,—is
not reached at all in these mountains. At twelve
thousand feet, it begins to lie in great patches on
the shaded sides of the hills, or in deep ravines,
and goes on to multiply in such form as the mountains rise to their greatest hight at fourteen thousand to fourteen thousand five hundred feet. But

it absolutely covers no mountain peak; the tops
of Gray's Peaks and Mount Lincoln, the highest
points in the whole region, are dry and bare, at
least at midday, through August, though in reaching them you may go over snow fields twenty or
thirty feet deep and miles long, though nearly
every morning's sun may glance brilliantly off the
freshly whitened peaks of all the high mountains in
sight, and though it makes everywhere and at all
times a significant feature in all the landscape
visions of the country.   The full mountains of
snow and the vast rivers of ice that belong to
Switzerland are not here, and are certainly missed
by the experienced mountain traveler; but for their
absence we have many compensations,—a more varied and richer verdure, a wider range of mountains,
with greater variety of form and color, these elevated
Parks, that have no parallel anywhere for curious
combination of landscape feature and beauty and
practical use, a climate in summer that fosters comfort and makes high mountain travel both much
more possible and agreeable, and an atmosphere
that, in purity and dryness, in inspiring influence
upon body and mind, can find no match in any part
of Europe, nor elsewhere in America.

The third or western great division of Colorado
is comparatively unknown.   Explorers have crossed
it here and there; adventurous miners have pene-
trated into this and that of its valleys; but it holds
no real population, and its character is known only
in a general way.   The great mountain ranges
shade down irregularly through it into the vast

interior basin of the West, instead of breaking off
almost abruptly, as they do on their eastern side,
into the level plains; the Grand, the White, the
Green and the Gunnison, the great feeders of the
Colorado of the West, slash freely through it, often
by narrow and unapproachable gorges, often too
through wide and rich valleys; many a high park,
with rough sage brush and tall grass, spreads itself
out, cold and dreary in the north, warmer and more
fertile in the south. Many a fable of rich mines,
of beautiful valleys, of broken and ruined mountains,—the debris of great conflicts of nature,—·
many a deep faith in untold wealth and unnum-
bered beauties do I hear of and about this section
of the territory; but the fact remains that it has
but few settlers and no especial history,—and I
gather the conclusion that it is in every way less
interesting to traveler, less enticing to speculator
or settler, than the middle and eastern divisions.
New and thorough explorations are in progress
through its lines; another year will add something
to our knowledge of its valleys and mountains; but·
for the present it is perhaps as much unknown land
as any section of equal size in the United States.

IV.

TRAVEL AMONG THE MOUNTAINS.

From Denver up into the Mountains—How the Honest Miners
Travel, and Colorado Families Make Summer Excursions—
The Clear Creek Valleys—The Scene of Beirstadt's Storm in
the Rocky Mountains—The Outfit for a Trip to Middle Park—
We Celebrate the Mule—The Upper Valley of Clear Creek,
and up the Mountain Side—The Flowers, the Shrubs, and the
Trees of the Higher Regions.

Top of Berthoud Pass, August, 1868.

Going into the mountains from Denver, the traveler has choice of several roads.   To the north he
passes up Boulder Creek to Boulder City and its
sub-villages and mining camps; more directly west
are the Clear Creek valley routes, one by Golden
City, and on to North Clear Creek, with Black
Hawk and Central City, that run into each other
and form the chief mining town of the territory,
and passing from here over to South Clear Creek,
with Idaho, Fall River, Mill City, Empire and
Georgetown on its line,—this being the daily stage
route, and the other, farther south, going up the
Mount Vernon road, and striking down into the
South Clear Creek valley below Idaho; while still
farther south, where Bear Creek and Turkey Creek

3

come out of the mountain range, is the road that
leads up and through the South Park country. At
this season all these roads are good,—for mountain
roads; in most part quite excellent and much trav-
eled, and kept in repair by tolls collected under
territorial charters. Fifty miles is the end of the
stage line and wagon road at Georgetown; and a
like distance on either road takes you into the
midst of the high mountains, and to the foot of
the continental range. The Boulder and both the
Clear Creek roads all connect by cross-roads in the
mountains; but there is no direct connection between the South Park and the upper Clear Creek
valleys save by trails. A tri-weekly stage-wagon
goes direct from Denver into the South Park
region to supply its villages with mails and carry
passengers.

All these roads introduce one delightfully to close
companionship with the mountain scenery,—first
through the long, wide prairie; then into narrow
valleys; occasionally a bold gorge or canyon and a
broken mountain; up and among and over high
hills, commanding majestic views of higher summits beyond; through little wooded parks or open
fields, where grain grows and flocks feed, and some-
body keeps "a ranch;" by lively streams with tan-
gles of willows and hops and clematis, and fruity
shrubs up the drier and higher banks; among
flowers everywhere, growing finer and plentier the
higher you climb; out and in forests of various
species of cotton-wood and evergreen, often brown
and dead through wasting fires that have swept the

hill-sides, or half cleared for the consuming rage of
the gold and silver furnaces, but still a rich possession of beauty and wealth for the country; under
a sun always searching with heat, but through an
atmosphere growing rarer and rarer and drier and
drier, and ever fresh and cool,—the day's ride is
thus a perpetual pleasure and surprise to the new-
comer.

We scattered in disorder on our first trip to the
mountains. The Vice-President and the Governor
took the stage and fulfilled several appointments
to make speeches. • Governor Hunt of the Territory made up a camping excursion for the young
ladies, with carriage, saddle-horses and outfit of
tents, blankets, cooking-stove and "grub" in bulk,
and moved leisurely up by the Mount Vernon road,
—reckless of time or taverns, and stopping where-
ever hunger or night overtook them. That patri-
arch of the country, General Pierce, and myself,
drove "a one-horse shay" by the same route; and
when we grew hungry, we picked out a brook and
a choice lot of grass, turned the horse loose for an
hour, and lay among the flowers and disposed of
huge piles of bread and butter and meat, that
we had brought with us, after the fashion of the
country. This independent camping habit is almost the rule with home travelers here. It grew
up with the necessities of the early settlements and
the roving, straggling ways of the miners. The
taverns are not now frequent or good; the climate
favors the outdoor life at this season; and with
provision in abundance, blankets, a coffee-pot, a

frying-pan, and a sack of flour and a side of bacon, either in a wagon, or packed on an extra horse, if you are journeying in the saddle, even pleasure-travelers find it much the more comfortable and decidedly the more independent mode, while to the old settler, and especially to a miner, it is altogether a matter of course.   One of these hangs his blanket and his coffee-pot and frying-pan, with a joint of meat and a bit of bread, around his saddle, and without extra animal or companion, is good for a week's journey among the mountains.   What he lacks for food he finds in the streams or woods, or buys at the occasional ranch, and at night a deserted cabin, which is nearly always at hand, where miners have been and are not, or a roadside tree and an open camp fire furnish him shelter and warmth.   He sleeps the sleep of the tired, and if it rains and he gets wet, the renewed fire dries him, and the climate never encourages colds.   So with the multiple of our single traveler; with companions conveniences and comforts increase, but the fashion is the same ; and whole families,— mothers and babies included,—will, with covered wagon and a saddle-horse or two, make a pleasure visit to the mountains, after this fashion, and live literally on the country for days and weeks, in delightful and refreshing companionship with Nature.   It was this sort of life that we were all entering upon, in all its strange novelty and stimulating influences.

We found the Clear Creek valleys generally brisk and beautiful.   Between mining and milling

and the late floods, the north one is terribly torn
to pieces, and looks rough and ragged.   Black
Hawk and Central City may be good places to
get gold in, but there can be no genuine homes
there.   The valley is too narrow, a mere ravine,
and all beauty is sacrificed to use ; though after
all beauty is truly use,—but to the mere use of
washing out gold.   Below and above, the valley
widens and is finer ; but over the divide on the
South Branch, there is a very charming country to
look upon and live in.   Below Idaho, gulch mining,
which is pretty lively and successful still, despoils
the prospect so far as man can ; but the dozen or
fifteen miles from Idaho up by Fall River, Mill
City and Empire to Georgetown, is quite the nicest
bit of the inhabited portion of the mountains.   The
valley is not wide, indeed you can heave a stone
across it in the narrower, and fire a rifle from hill
to hill at its wider parts ; but it breaks out frequently into little nooks of plateaus or bars ; it
opens up into seductive side valleys or canyons,
and it winds and turns about, and sends up its
high mountain walls in form and manner, to present a constantly varying but ever beautiful scene.
At the upper end, winter confronts you in snow-
covered peaks ; below, nature looks warm and sum-
mer-like ; and though the valley is from seven thousand five hundred to eight thousand five hundred
feet high, the days are like June and October, and
the winter is not long or severe.   Till you reach
Georgetown, where the hills shut in the valley
sharply, and the rich silver section has its center,

there is not much mining, and the villages are but neighborhoods of six to a dozen houses each. Idaho and Fall River have good hotels, and are favorite summer resorts. The former has a wonderful hot soda spring that furnishes most refreshing and health-giving baths. Over it rise a family group of three peaks, distinguishable in all mountain views, and known as the Chief, Squaw and Papoose, and up from the valley here you rise to Chicago Lake and Chicago Mountain, familiar as the foreground scene in Bierstadt's "Storm in the Rocky Mountains."

All these mountains go sharply up from two to four thousand feet above the valley, often past the timber line, and end in snow or bare, grim rocks. They offer unending fascination to the lover of mountain-climbing and mountain views ; while to lie on the grassy banks just above the river,—that, in practical parenthesis, it should be noted, runs swift and strong down the rapid descent of the valley, and is full of "water power,"—in the warm sun, and look through the snowy fleece of grasshoppers, that with outstretched wings fill the air, up and among them,—masses of forest and rock and patches of snow,—to the line of brightened blue sky they border,—this is just comfort and rest, and is worth the coming to experience.

It was from here that, sending wagons and women, tents and trunks, back to Denver, and coming down as the miners say to the "bed-rock" of flannel overshirts and a pocket comb for personal baggage, we started with a select masculine party for a week's trip over into the Middle Park.

We had a number of welcome Colorado volunteers for this expedition. There were a full dozen of us that gathered after breakfast on mule and horseback in the last camp of Governor Hunt and the young ladies, far up the Clear Creek valley, above Empire. The latter went back, we forward, led by Governor Hunt and Indian Agent Oakes. Charley Utter, a famous mountaineer, trapper, Indian scout, rover, such a character as only the American border can breed, small and tough, wiry and witty, intelligent and handsome,—alike at home in your parlor or an Indian hut,—and to whom all these mountains and parks are as familiar as your own paternal acres are to yourself; he and his assistant, Franklin Ashley, provided our animals and outfit generally, and also came along with us, to guide and help us in our new and strange life. Two extra mules and a horse carried our blankets and provisions and cooking utensils, and the personal baggage of those not weaned yet from carpet bags.

Some experience as a traveler myself, and more valuable advice from those of larger, had taught me to rise superior to such aristocratic impediments. Indeed, it proved I was outfitted in quite a model way, and had more of what was necessary and less of what was not, than others of the inexperienced in camp and mountain travel. First, woolen stockings and winter under clothing; and of these, an extra set, with two extra handkerchiefs and two towels, soap, comb and tooth-brush and slippers, only moderately filled a pair of light saddle-bags on my own animal. Over the undershirt was worn a dark and thick cassimere shirt, with turnover collar of same and pocket in breast, which, coming nowhere in contact with the body, may be worn for weeks without disrespect to your washerwoman. A pair of very thick, high top, riding boots, of extra size, my last winter's thick pantaloons and heavy sack coat, and an old soft hat, flexible as a rag, and answering as well for a nightcap, completed my clothing. No vest or waistcoat, no suspenders; a strap around the waist held things together, and carried a revolver and a tin cup. Over the saddle-bags behind were strapped a thin woolen overcoat,—it better have been thick, —and a loose rubber cloth coat; both which were frequently in use, and were always valuable at night; and as often in mid-day they had the company around the saddle of the sack coat, and I rode under the warm sun in pantaloons and shirts. It was a neat, complete and compact personal outfit; everything that was needed for a trip of two or three weeks, and the only modification I would make, in going again, would be to substitute a pair of old shoes for the slippers, and to have the rubber overcoat so modified that it would closely cover the legs in the saddle down to the boot-tops. All this was carried on and around my own saddle; my bedding alone went on the pack animals, and this consisted of two pairs of heavy blankets, a buffalo robe, a rubber blanket and a pillow,—all strapped into a tight roll or bundle,—no more than one restless sleeper needs in the cold nights of these outdoor mountains, but equally abundant for two square and fair sleepers who will turn over at one and the same time and don't kick the clothes off.

My mule,—did you ever ride a mule? There is no other experience that exactly fits one for this. As far as a mule's brains go, he is pretty sensible, —and so obstinate! But it takes a long while to beat a new idea into his head, and when it dawns on him, the effect is so overpowering that he just stops in amazed bewilderment, and won't move on again until he is relieved of the foreign conscious-ness, and gets back to his own original possessions. The whole process is startlingly human; it inspires you with faith in the idea of the transmigration of souls. I know *so* many people who must have been mules once, or will be,—else there is no vir-tue in the fitness of things! But my mule be-longed to the best of the race; he was prudent,— he never went in any doubtful places until some-body else had gone before and proved the way; he was very patient,—he would always stop for me to get off, or to get on; he was very tough,—my spurs never seemed to annoy him one atom, and my rid-ing him didn't wear any skin off of *his* backsides, not a bit. But after we grew acquainted, and he came to appreciate the more delicate shades of my char-acter, we got on charmingly together for the first half of the day; in the afternoon, when he grew lazy and tired, and I nervous, we often had serious discussions,—sometimes with sticks,—but he gen-erally got the best of the argument.

If a well-broken Indian pony or a "broncho"

(a California half-breed horse) can be got, either is
probably better than a mule ; more springy in tread
and quicker in movement, and equally careful in
mountain-climbing and fording streams and ditches ;
but otherwise, the mule is the better animal for your
work on these expeditions.   A "States" horse can't
stand the hard riding and tough climbing, and besides must have grain to keep him up, while the mule
and the Indian and "broncho" ponies will live on the
rich grasses of the country.   The latter are apt to
be wilful and wicked, and should only be taken, in
preference to the mules, upon good references as to
character and a trial to boot.

But "get up, Jenny."   We are falling fast in the
rear.   The narrow valley rapidly narrows, and becomes a defile, a gorge, wooded and flowered, rock-
strewed and briskly watered,—a wild Alpine scene.
The mountains rise sharp and sheer, one thousand
and two thousand feet above the road, and wide
walls of red granite hang over it.   The stream
turns and twists and foams, and we follow a half-
made road along, over, in its rugged path.   There
was an attempt made a few years ago to build a
stage road through the mountains and over into
Utah by this route; many thousand dollars were
spent upon it; but it was found too big a job, and
it is passable now for only a few miles farther on.
It takes the traveler into and among rich mountain beauties; even to come up here and go back,
without an objective point beyond, is abundant
recompense.

After four or five miles of this road, we turn

sharply from it up an abrupt mountain trail; in single file, along a mere path on a steep hill-side, a mis-step of the mule would send animal and rider rolling over and over among the sparse trees down the declivity,—but mules don't mis-step, and even the top-heavy pack jacks,—a mountain on a mole-hill, indeed,—carried their burden and themselves unharmed to the top. The thin and thinning air offered severer trial, however, and the beasts strug-gled like huge bellows for wind, and trembled be-neath us in the effort to take in enough to keep going; to get off and walk was to undergo the same trial ourselves, and walking or riding, we had every few rods to stop and adjust the lungs of man and beast to the rare and growing rarer air. There was temptation to stop, too, in the widening view of the upper mountains; their snowy fields and gray or red or brown walls and peaks lifted into sight, on all sides, close and familiar, distant and stranger, but making us feel, for the first time, their real companionship,—that nearness to great and sublime nature that awes and uplifts like the presence of God himself.

Passing the sharp mountain side, we come, at a hight of ten thousand feet, to pleasant little park openings, ascending by easy grade, half-wooded, and whose bright grass and abundant flowers and deep evergreens tell of fertile soil and protecting hights around. Such spots are frequent in all these high mountain ranges, and are exceeding fair to look upon. They are in their glory at this season; it is but a little while back to last year's snows, and

a few weeks forward to another wintry embrace;
and they make the most of their stinted time. So
in July and August they compress the growth and
the blossom of the whole year; and we see at
once flowers that are passed and flowers that are
yet to come in the Plains below; dandelions and
buttercups, violets and roses, larkspurs and harebells, painter's brush and blue gentian,—these and
their various companions of spring, summer and
autumn, here they all are, starring the grass, drooping over the brook, improving every bit of sunshine
among the trees, jealous of every lost hour in their
brief lives.

I wish I could repeat the roll of this army of
beauties for the benefit of my flower-learned readers; I know most of them very well by sight, as
the lad said of his unlearned alphabet, but cannot
call them by name. Blue and yellow are the dominant colors; of the former several varieties of little
bell and trumpet-shaped blossoms, pendant along
stalwart stalks; again, a similar shaped flower, but
more delicate,—a little tube in pink and white,
seems original here; and of the golden hues, there
are babies and grand-babies of the sun-flower family in every shade and shape. One of these, about
the size of a small tea-saucer, holds a center stem
or spike of richest maroon red, with deepest yellow
leaves flaring away from it,—each color the very
concentration and ripeness of itself, as if dyed at
the very fountain head. The harebell is at home
everywhere; drooping modestly and alone on the
barren and exposed mountain side at eleven thou-

sand or twelve thousand feet, as well as in the protected parks among all its rivals; but the fringed
gentian is more fastidious, and grows only where
nature is richer, but then in such masses, with
such deep blueness and such undeviating upright-
ness of stem, as to prove its birthright here. The
painter's brush, as familiarly called here, is a new
flower to me; something like the soldier's pompon
in form, it stands stiff and distinct on a single
stalk, about six inches tall, with three inches' length
and one inch in thickness or diameter of flower, in
every shade of red from deepest crimson to pale
pink, and again in straw colors from almost white
to deep lemon. We picked on a single morning's
ride seven of different shades of red. A bunch of
the brightest of this flower, with sprinkling of those
of milder hues and a few grasses, such as could be
gathered in five minutes in many a patch of Alpine
meadow we passed through, was enough to set a
flower-lover crazy with delight. It was a beacon,
a flame of color, and would make a room aglow like
brilliant picture or wood fire on the hearth. But
perhaps the most bewitching of the flowers we discovered was a columbine, generous but delicate, of
pale but firm purple and pure white,—it was very
exquisite in form and shading. Higher up, where
only mosses could grow for rock and snow, these
were in great variety and richness, with white, with
blue and with pink blossoms.

All this wonderful wealth and variety of flower
is marked with strength but not coarseness; the
colors are more deep and delicate than are found in

garden flowers; and though frost and snow may stiffen their blossoms every morning,—for at ten thousand feet high and above, the temperature must go down to freezing every night,—the dryness of the air preserves them through their season, and they keep on growing and flowering until their September and October winter fairly freezes them out.

There is no such variety and beauty in the forests of the Rocky Mountains as those of the East and the extreme West both offer. The oak, the maple, the elm, the birch, all hard woods are unknown. Pines, firs and spruces of various species, and the cotton-wood, a soft maple or poplar, with delicate white wood and a pale green and smooth leaf, are all that this region can offer for trees. Nor are these generally of large size. The forests seem young and the individual trees small, even by the side of those of New England; there is no hint among them of the giants of the Pacific coast. The probability is that they are young, that the Indians kept them well burned off, and that, with settlement and civilization, in spite of the wanton waste now in progress, and against which there should be some speedy protection, the forest wealth will increase. Perhaps not in these first years, but by and by, when coal takes the chief place for fuel, and self-interest and legislation work out their care of the trees, and prevent devastating fires. But many a fine grove of thick and tall pines, that would warm the heart of any ship-builder, have we passed through; and their deep colors and firm forms, contrasting with the light and free-moving cotton-wood, give a pleasing and animated life to the forest landscape.

But the silver spruce is the one gem of the trees; a sort of first cousin of the evergreen we call the balsam fir in our New England yards, but more richly endowed with beauty of shape and color. It is scattered plentifully through these mountain valleys, and looks as if a delicate silver powder had been strewn over its deep green needles, or rather as if a light white frost had fallen all upon and enshrouded it; and you cannot help wondering why the breeze does not shake the powder off, or the sun dissipate the frost, so ever present is the one illusion or the other. But it holds its birthright persistently,—a soft white-blue-green combination of positive power that comes into the rather hardish gray neutral coloring of the general landscape with most agreeable, even inspiriting effects. This and another spruce often throw themselves into a very charming form of growth; gathering around an old pine, they will shoot up numerous spires, thin and tall, thicker and shorter, and so shade down to a close, spreading mass in a wide semicircle around,—a bit of natural cathedral-like posturing in tree and shrub life, so often repeated as to suggest art, so effective as to call out the delight and envy of every landscape artist who sees it. Everywhere among these high mountains, in barren rather than in fertile spots, we unexpectedly find the "Mahonia Holly," a favorite but winter dying shrub of our eastern lawns; they call it here the Oregon grape, for it bears a little berry, and it is evidently killed to the root every winter, for it gets only a few inches of growth, and I do not find it massed at all. But in its freely scattered little specimens, its deep, smooth and hard green leaves kept company with us until we had passed the timber line, and come out among the snow fields.

V.

THE MIDDLE PARK.

The Berthoud Pass—"Such a Getting Down" Hill—Our First
Night in Camp—The Middle Park and Across it—An Indian
Rescue and a Civilized Reception—The Mountain Raspberries
—The Hot Douche Springs—Trout Fishing—Life with the
Ute Indians.

HOT SPRINGS, Middle Park, August, 1868.

AFTER three or four hours' hard riding, from the
upper Clear Creek, we suddenly came out of the
trees into an open space of hardy green, bordered
by snow, a gap or sag in the mountains,—and behold we are at the top of Berthoud Pass. The
waters of the Atlantic and Pacific start from our
very feet; the winds from the two oceans suck
through here into each other's embrace; above us
the mountain peaks go up sharp with snow and
rock, and shut in our view; but below and beyond
through wide and thick forests lies Middle Park, a
varied picture of plain and hill, with snowy peaks
beyond and around. To this point, at least, I would
advise all pleasure travelers to Colorado to come;
it is a feasible excursion for any one who can sit in
the saddle; it can be easily made with return in a
day from Empire, Georgetown or even Idaho; and

it offers as much of varied and sublime beauty in
mountain scenery, as any so comparatively easy a
trip yet within our experience possibly can.

• But to follow us down into the Park is another
and tougher affair; the Colorado ladies do it occasionally, but it needs real strength and endurance
and an unfaltering enthusiasm. The descent is
sharp and rocky, and thick with timber, and worse,
wet and miry. Bayard Taylor, who came over in
June, found the path heavy with snow, and impassable to any but heroic travelers; now the snows
are gone, and it is dryer than at any other season,
but it is a rough and hard descent, almost perpendicular in steepness at times, and full of treacherous
holes of water and mire. But we all got through
without disaster, and found relief about two o'clock
in an open, grassy meadow, with a trout brook on its
border. The order to camp was grateful; animals
were turned loose, and we lolled in the sunshine,
made and drank coffee, and ate our lunch of bread
and butter, ham and canned peaches.

But we were not in the Park yet, and after an
hour's rest, we remounted and moved on,—on,
on, the road seemed interminable, through thick
woods, over frequent morass and occasional mountain stream; deceptive in glimpse of park that was
not the Park; all, save our irrepressible mountain
leaders, weary with the long, rough ride, and eager
for the end. It was near dark, after traveling from
twenty to twenty-five miles in all, when we stopped
for the night, in the woods, just without the open
section of the Park. A bit of meadow with tall

grass was at hand for the animals, and, relieved of
saddles and packs, away they went, without let or
hindrance, to enjoy it. The only precaution taken
is to leave the lariat, a rope of twenty to thirty feet
long, dragging at their necks, by which to catch
them the more easily in the morning. Only a portion of the herd are thus provided, however. They
rarely stray away far from camp; and if they should,
these people make little of an hour or two's hunt to
find them, which they are quite sure of doing wher-
ever the best grass grows. The animals are picketed only when there is danger from the Indians,
or a prompt start is necessary.

A big fire is soon blazing; a part prepare the
supper,—tea and coffee, bacon, trout, potatoes good
bread and butter, and, to-night, a grouse soup, the
best use Governor Hunt can make of an old bird
he shot on the road, to-day, and very good use it
proved, too, by help of tin pail, potatoes and butter;
—others feed the fire, bring the water, and prepare
the camp for sleeping. An old canvass cloth serves
for table; we squat on our blankets around it, and
with tin cups, tin plates, knife and fork and spoon,
take what is put before us, and are more than content. Eating rises to a spiritual enjoyment after
such a day; and the Trois Freres or Delmonico does
not offer a "squarer meal" than Governor Hunt.
The "world's people" make their beds against a
huge tree, and cut and plant boughs around the
heads to keep out the cold wind; but the old camp-
ers drop their blankets anywhere around the fire;
and after going back over the day and forward to

the morrow in pleasant chat, sitting around the glowing mass of flame and coal, we crawl in under our blankets, in a grand circle about the now smouldering logs, say our prayers to the twinkling stars up through the trees, and,—think of those new spring beds invented in Springfield!

We broke up housekeeping and started into the Park by nine o'clock the next morning. It isn't an easy matter to make an earlier start, when we have to carry our homes with us; cook and eat breakfast; wash the dishes; catch the animals; pack up beds and provisions; clean up camp, and reconstruct not only for a day's journey, but for a family moving. A short ride brought us into miles of clear prairie, with grass one to two feet high, and hearty streams struggling to be first into the Pacific Ocean. This was the Middle Park, and we had a long twenty-five miles ride northerly through it that day. It was not monotonous by any means. Frequent ranges of hills break the prairie; the latter changes from rich bottom lands with heavy grass, to light, cold gravelly uplands, thin with bunch grass and sage bush; sluggish streams and quick streams alternate; belts of hardy pines and tender looking aspens (cotton-wood) lie along the crests or sides of hills; farther away are higher hills fully wooded, and still beyond, "the range" that bounds the Park and circles it with eternal snows. The sun shines warm; there are wide reddish walls of granite or sandstone along many of the hills; some of the intervales are rich with green grass; and the sky is deep blue; and yet the prevailing tone and impression of the Park is a coldish gray. You find it on the earth; you see it in the subdued, tempered, or faded greens of leaf and shrub and grass; it hangs over the distant mountains; it prevails in the rocks; you feel it in the air,—a certain sort of stintedness or withholding impresses you, amid the magnificence of distance, of hight and breadth and length, with which you are surrounded, and which is the first and greatest and most constant thought of the presence.

We scattered along wildly enough; some stopping to catch trout; others humoring lazy mules and horses; others to enjoy at leisure the novel surroundings,—meeting, with fellow-feeling, for lunch and the noon rest, but dividing again for the afternoon ride. All had gone before,—leaders, guides, packs, and were out of sight,—when my friend and especial companion on this trip, Mr. Hawkins of Mill City, of Springfield raising and relation, and myself rose over the hill that looked down into the valley that was our destination. It was a broad, fine vision. Right and. left, several miles apart, ran miniature mountain ranges,—before, six miles away, rose an abrupt gray mountain wall; just beneath it, through green meadow, ran the Grand River; up to us a smooth, clean, gradual ascent; along the river bank, a hundred white tents, like dots in the distance, showed the encampment of six to eight hundred Ute Indians, awaiting our party with "heap hungry" stomachs; in the upper farther corner, under the hill-side, a faint mist and steam in the air located the famous

Hot Springs of the Middle Park,—the whole as complete a picture of broad, open plain, set in mountain frame, as one would dream of. It spurred our lagging spirits, and we galloped down the long plane, whose six miles seemed to the eye not a third so long in this dry, pure air.

Reaching the river, through the Indian encampment, whose mongrel curs alone gave fighting greeting, it looked deep and was boisterous; our animals hesitated; and we thought sympathetically of Bayard Taylor's sad fortune in making this hard journey into the Middle Park to see and try the Hot Springs, and then being obliged by the flood to content himself with a distant view from this bank of the river. But our comrades had gone over; and the only question was where. Looking for their track, directly there came galloping to our relief a gayly costumed Indian princess,—we were sure she was,—bare-backed for her haste to succor, and full of sweet sympathy for our anxiety, and tender smiles for our—attractiveness in misfortune. Plunging boldly into what seemed to us the deepest and swiftest part of the stream,—as doubtless it was,—she beckoned us to follow, with every enticing expression of eye and lips and hand; and follow we, of course, did,—had it been more dangerous we should,—and by folding ourselves up on the highest parts of our animals, we got through without serious wetting. But it proved that we crossed in the wrong place, and that our beautiful Indian princess, with beads and feathers and bright eyes and seductive ways, was only a plain young

" buck,"—not even a maiden, not so much as a
squaw, not, to come down to the worst at once, so
near to glory and gallantry as a relationship to the .
Chief.   Nothing less than the welcome we had
from one of the best women of Colorado,—whom
we parted from last in Fifth Avenue, and now
found spending the summer with her family in a
log cabin of one room, with eight hundred Indians
for her only neighbors,—and the arrival of her
husband from his afternoon's fishing with two
bushels of fine trout packed over his horse's back,
—here only was adequate soothing and consolation
for our chagrin.   And we didn't go into camp that
night till after supper,—after supper of fresh biscuits, fried trout, and mountain raspberries!

Let me celebrate these high mountain raspberries before the taste goes from my mouth.
They grow freely on the hill-sides, from seven
thousand to ten thousand feet up, on bushes
from six to eighteen inches high, are small and
red, and the only wild fruit of the region worth
eating.   They are delicate and high-flavored to
extreme ; their mountain home refines and elevates them into the very concentration and essence of all fruitiness ; they not only tickle. but
intoxicate the palate,—so wild and aromatic, indeed, are they·that they need some sugar to tone
the flavor down to the despiritualized sense ˙of a
cultivated taste.   Yet they are not so sour as to
require sweetening,—only too high-toned for the
stranger stomach ; after sharing their native˙ air
a few days, we found them best picked and eaten

from the vines. It is one of the motives of family excursion parties into the mountains at this season to lay in a supply of raspberry jam for the year; while the men catch trout, the women pick raspberries, cook and sugar them in the camp-kettle, and go home laden with this rare fruity sweetmeat. Here in the Middle Park we were kept in full supply of the fresh fruit by the Ute squaws, who, going off into the hills in the morning, often two together astride the same pony, and a little papoose strapped on its board over the back of one, would come back at night with cups and pails of the berries to exchange with the whites for their own two great weaknesses, sugar and biscuit. But the bears get the most of the raspberries so far. They are at home with them during all the season, and can pick and eat at leisure.

The Hot Springs of the Middle Park are both a curiosity and a virtue. They are a considerable resort already by Coloradians at this season, and when convenient roads are made over into the Park, there will be a great flow of visitors to them. We found twenty or thirty other visitors here, scattered about in the neighborhood, while parties were coming and going every day. The springs for bathing, and the rivers for fishing, are the two great attractions. On the hill-side, fifty feet above the Grand River, and a dozen rods away, these hot sulphurous waters bubble up at three or four different places within a few feet, and coming together into one stream flow over an abrupt bank, say a dozen feet high, into a little circular pool or basin below.

Thence the waters scatter off into the river. But the pool and the fall unite to make a charming natural bathing-house. You are provided with a hot sitz bath and douche together. The stream that pours over the precipice into the pool is about as large as would flow out of a full water pail turned over, making a stream three to five inches in diameter. The water is so hôt that you cannot at first bear your hand in it, being 110° Fahrenheit in temperature, and the blow of the falling water and its almost scalding heat send the bather shrieking out on his first trial of them; but with light experiments, first an arm, then a leg, and next a shoulder, he gradually gets accustomed to both heat and fall, and can stand directly under the stream without flinching, and then he has such a bath as he can find nowhere else in the world. The invigorating effects are wonderful; there is no lassitude, no chill from it, as is usually experienced after an ordinary hot bath elsewhere; though the water be 110° warm, and the air 30° to 40° cold, the shock of the fall is such a tonic, and the atmosphere itself is so dry and inspiring, that no reaction, no unfavorable effects are felt, even by feeble persons, in coming from one into the other. The first thing in the morning, the last at night did we renew our trial of this hot douche bath during our brief stay in the neighborhood, and the old grew young and the young joyous and rampant from the experience. Wonderful cures are related as having been effected by these springs; the Indians resort to them a good deal, put their sick horses into them, and are loth to yield control of them to the whites; and in view of their probable future value, there has been a struggle among the latter for their ownership. They are now in the hands of Mr. Byers of the Rocky Mountain News at Denver, under a title that will probably defy all disputants. The waters look and taste precisely like those of the Sharon Sulphur Springs in New York. The difference is that these are hot, those cold. They have deposited sulphur, iron and soda in quantity all about their path, and these are their probable chief ingredients.

Over a little hill from the springs, by the side of the Grand River,—the hill, the stream, and a half mile between us and the Indian encampment,—we settled down in camp for two days and a half, studying Indian life, catching and eating trout, taking hot douche baths in the springs, and making excursions over the neighboring hills into side valleys. The river before us offered good fishing, but better was to be found in Williams Fork, a smaller stream a few miles below, where a half day's sport brought back from forty-to sixty pounds of as fine speckled trout as ever came from brooks or lakes of New England. They ranged from a quarter of a pound up to two pounds weight each, and we had them at every meal.

The Indians were very neighborly; hill, stream and distance were no impediment to their attentions; their ponies would gallop with them over all in five minutes; and from two to a dozen, men and boys, never the squaws, were hanging about our camp fires from early morning till late evening.

Curiosity, begging and good-fellowship were their only apparent motives; they did no mischief; they stole nothing, though food and clothing, pistols and knives, things they coveted and needed above all else, were loosely scattered about within reach; they only became a nuisance by being everlastingly in the way and spoiling the enjoyment of one's food by their wistful observation. Mrs. Browning says, you remember, that observation, which is not sympathy, is simply torture. And not a bit of sympathy did they show in our eating except as they shared. We were as liberal as our limited stores would allow; but the capacity of a single Indian's stomach is boundless; what could we do for the hundreds?

These Utes are a good deal higher grade of Indian than I had supposed. They are above the average of our Indian tribes in comeliness and intelligence; and none perhaps are better behaved or more amenable to direction from the whites. There are seven different bands or tribes of them, who occupy the mountains and parks of Colorado and adjoining sections of New Mexico and Utah. The bands number from five hundred to one thousand each. This one consisted of about seventy-five "lodges" or families, each represented by a tent of cloth stretched over a bunch of poles gathered at the top, and spreading around in a small circle. The poles leave a hole in the top for the smoke of a fire in the center beneath, and around which the family squat on their blankets and pile their stores of food and skins and clothing. Probably there

were six hundred in the camp near us, men, women
and children.   They look frailer and feebler than
you would expect; I did not see a single Indian
who was six feet high or would weigh over one
hundred and seventy-five pounds; they are all, indeed, under size, and no match in nervous or physical force for the average white man.   Some of both
sexes are of very comely appearance, with fine hands
and delicate feet, and shapely limbs, with a bright
mulatto complexion, and clear, piercing eyes; but
their square heads, coarse hair, hideous daubs of
yellow and red paint on the cheek and forehead,
and motley raiment,—here a white man's cast-off
hat, coat or pantaloons, if squaw a shabby old gown
of calico or shirt of white cloth, alternate with Indian leggins and moccasins, bare legs and feet, a
dirty white or flaming red blanket, beaded jacket
of leather, feathers, and brass or tin trinkets hanging on the head, from the ears, down the back or
breast,—all these disorderly and unaccustomed combinations give them at first a repulsive and finally
a very absurd appearance.   The squaws seem to
be kept in the background, and, except when brides
or the wives of a chief, dress much more plainly
and shabbily than the bucks.   They are all more
modest and deferential in appearance and manners
than would be expected; and I saw no evidence of
or taste for strong drink among this tribe,—none
of them ever asked for it, while their desire for food,
especially for sugar and biscuit, was always manifest.   The sugar they gobble up without qualification, and such unnatural food as this and fine flour

breed diseases and weaknesses that are already de-
stroying the race. Coughs are frequent, and dys-
pepsia ; sickness and deaths are quite common
among the children ; and this incongruous mixture
of white man's food and raiment and life with their
own, which their contact with civilization has led
them into, is sapping their vitality at its fountains.
To make matters the worse, they have got hold of
our quack medicines, and are great customers for
Brandreth and other pills, with the vain hope of
curing their maladies. In short, they are simple,
savage children, and in that definition we find suggested the only proper way for the government to
treat them.

Their wealth consists in their horses, which they
breed or steal from their enemies of other tribes,
and of which this tribe in the Middle Park must
have a couple of hundred. They live on the game
they can find in the parks and among the mountains, moving from one spot to another, as seasons
and years change, the proceeds of the skins of the
deer and other animals they kill, roots, nuts and
berries, and the gifts of the government and the
settlers. It is altogether even a precarious and
hard reliance ; the game is fast disappearing,—save
of trout we have not seen enough in all our travels among the mountains to feed our small party
upon, if it had all been caught ; and the government agents are not always to be depended upon
in making up deficiencies. Our neighbors had
lately come over from the North Park, where they
had hunted antelope to some purpose and with

rare fortune, killing four thousand in all in two or three weeks, half of them in a single grand hunt. They cut the meat into thin slices and dry it, so that it looks like strips of old leather; and as we went about their camp we saw the little, weakly children pulling away at bits of it, apparently with not very satisfactory results. Our tribe was in trouble about a chief; the old one was dead, and there were two or three contestants for the succession; but the wrangle was not half so fierce as would arise over a contested election for mayor of a white man's city.

Affairs always seemed very quiet in the Indian camp in the day-time; the braves played cards, or did a little hunting; the squaws gathered wood, tanned skins, braided lariats, or made fantastic leather garments; the boys chased the ponies; but at night they as invariably appeared to be having a grand pow-wow,—rude music and loud shouting rolled up to our camp a volume of coarse sound that at first seemed frightful, as if the preparatory war-whoop for a grand scalping of their white neighbors, but which we learned to regard as the most innocent of barbaric amusements. Though these Utes are quite peaceful and even long-suffering towards the whites, they bear eternal enmity to the Indian tribes of the Plains, and are always ready to have a fight with them. Each party is strongest on its own territory,—the Arapahoes, Comanches and Cheyennes on the prairies, and the Utes among the hills; and each, while eager rarely go a-visiting. The Plains Indians are better mounted and better armed; chiefly because, keeping up nearly constant warfare with the whites, they have exacted prompter presents and larger pay from the government. The Utes complain, and with reason, that their friendliness causes them to be neglected and cheated; while their and our enemies thrive on government bounty.

There is now a plan for all the Ute tribes to go together into the south-western corner of Colorado, away from the mines and the whites, and there, upon abundant pastures and fruitful mountains, engage in a pastoral and half agricultural life; to set up stock-raising on a large scale, and such tillage as they can bring themselves to, under the protection and aid of the government. The scheme is a good one; the Indians agree to it; and the bargain has been made by the government agents here,—all that is needed is for the authorities at Washington to furnish the means for carrying it into execution. So far as our observation extends, the greatest trouble with our Indian matters lies at Washington; the chief of the cheating and stupidity gathers there; while the Indian agents here upon the ground are, if not immaculate, certainly more intelligent, sensible, and practical, and truer to the good of the settler and the Indian than their superiors at the seat of government.

VI.

FROM MIDDLE PARK BY BOULDER PASS.

The Longing Lingering in Middle Park—Professor Powell and his
Explorations—The Canyon of the Colorado—Over the Boulder
Pass in a Snow Storm—A Cold Night and a Warm Noon Camp
—Night in a Barn—By Boulder and Central to Mill City and
Georgetown.

MILL CITY, Colorado, August, 1868.

WE were loth to leave the Middle Park. I
counted the hot douche sulphur baths, and tried
to multiply them by six, then by two; but it was
of no use,—the Vice-President travels by time-
table; and the ladies were in Denver, and the
grand expedition to South Park was ahead. I
looked longingly through the hills up the valley
of the Grand; beyond I knew there lay a wilder
country than we had seen, and under the shadow
of Long's Peak, Grand Lake itself, a large and fine
sheet of water, alive with trout, and rich in commanding beauty. We galloped over the bare hills
the other way, and looked off down the valley.
Bits of rare stone, agates and jaspers and crystals
and petrifactions, lay everywhere about; and over
the river, a dozen miles off, was the famous "moss
agate patch," where these peculiar crystallizations
covered the ground; Williams Fork came rollick-

ing down the opposite hill-sides through a line of trees, with innumerable breakfasts of uncaught trout, and a wide green meadow at the mouth for camping ground; while far on in the landscape, the Grand found magnificent pathway for twenty-five miles through a broad field of heavy grass,—the gem, the kernel of the Middle Park; then turning abruptly west, it shot through the mountains by a canyon, lapped up the Blue on the other side, and, thus strengthened, poured out southward for the Colorado and the Pacific Ocean.   It was this way we should have gone out,—down the Grand and up the Blue, all within the capacious boundaries of the Middle Park,—but time and the provision bag forbade.   Yet there was nothing inviting in the return by the Berthoud Pass; there could be nothing worse than its mire and its rough ascent; another way would at least be new,—and we voted to go out by its rival for a railroad track, the Boulder Pass.   The Governor (Hunt) and the Indian agent, finding their talk with the Indians not eloquent enough to convince by lack of food and blankets, had gone back by the old route, taking a dozen or twenty of the leading braves with them, to seek arguments where the freight was not so expensive.   The Indian sees the point of an idea always through a full stomach and a warm back, and it required a whole beef and several barrels of flour and sugar and a dozen blankets to prove to them that a petty technical amendment by the Senate to their last treaty was just right.

We had made familiar and friendly acquaintance

with Professor Powell's scientific exploring party,
from Illinois, while in the Middle Park.   They were
in camp there for some time, and made it the end
of their summer and the beginning of their winter
campaign. The party comprises a dozen or more
enthusiastic young men, interested in one department or other of natural science, or eager for border experiences, mostly from Illinois, and giving
their time and labor to the expedition for the sake
of the education and the health.   Professor Powell,
the originator and head, does more·; the government furnishes food, allowing it to be drawn from
the supplies of the nearest post, and the Illinois
University and Natural History Society contribute
small sums of money; but he draws upon his private purse for all deficiencies, and these must be
many thousands of dollars before he gets through.
The summer has been spent among the higher
Mountains and in the Parks, taking careful notes
with barometer and thermometer, collecting flowers
and birds and larger animals, and studying the rare
geological phenomena of the country.   Their collection of birds is very full and valuable, and numbers over two hundred different specimens.

Professor Powell, two or three of his assistants,
and Mr. Byers, of the Denver News, who knows all
these mountains better than any other man, probably, have just accomplished the ascent of Long's
Peak.   This is the prominent north-eastern mountain of the Coloradian series, is seen from the Railroad, and is fourteen thousand feet high, and has
heretofore defied all the efforts of explorers and

mountaineers to reach its top. They had a terribly hard climb of it, but felt amply paid in the glory of the fact, and more in the glory of the landscape spread before them at the summit. The plains and mountains to the north beyond the Railroad, the unending eastern plains, with Denver and the intervening settlements below and to the south, the whole of Middle Park, and the surrounding and far-beyond mountains,—all Colorado, as it were, and part of Wyoming, lay beneath their eyes. Streams flowed out from the mountain in all directions, and no fewer than thirty-nine lakes on that and the neighboring mountain sides, nearly all of and above the altitude of ten thousand feet, were visible from their commanding hight.

From here the explorers will follow down the Grand River, out of the Park into western Colorado, and then strike across to the other and larger branch of the great Colorado River, the Green, and upon that or some of its branches, near the line of Utah, spend the winter in camp, studying up their past achievements, and preparing for the next summer's campaign. The great and final object of the expedition is to explore the upper Colorado River and solve the mysteries of its three hundred mile canyon. They will probably undertake this next season by boats and rafts from their winter camp on the Green; but they may postpone the adventure till another year, and meantime discover and reveal the mountains and plains of western Colorado and eastern Utah, which are so little known. But the mocking ignorance and fascinating reports

of the course and country of the Colorado ought
to hasten them to this interesting field. The maps
from Washington, that put down only what is absolutely, scientifically known, leave a great blank space
here of three hundred to five hundred miles long
and one hundred to two hundred miles broad. Is
any other nation so ignorant of itself? All that
we do know goes to show that, beginning with the
union of the Grand and the Green Rivers, the Colorado is confined for three hundred miles within perpendicular walls of rock averaging three thousand
feet high, up which no one can climb, down which
no one can safely go, and between which in the
river, rapids and falls and furious eddies render
passage frightful, certainly dangerous, possibly impossible.

The general conviction of the border population
is that whoever dares venture into this canyon will
never come out alive. But we have an authentic
account this season of a man who made the trip
last year and lives to tell the tale. He and a companion, prospecting for gold in south-western Colorado, and driven by Indians, took to the Grand
River just before its union with the Green, made
a raft and committed themselves to the waters.
Foaming rapids and a whirlpool swept the companion and all the provisions off, and they were
lost, while White, the surviving hero's name, without food, passed seven days more, a second seven
days, upon these strange waters, between frowning
walls, over dangerous rapids, through delaying eddies, before he reached Callville in Arizona, the

first settlement and the head of navigation on the
river.   His entire journey upon the river must
have exceeded five hundred miles, and he repre-
sents that for most of the distance it was through
these traditional high walls, impassable as a for-
tress, a dungeon over a cataract.

Nearly all of the rivers of Colorado and Utah run
for brief distances, from one to twenty-five miles,
through these gorges of rock; or they "canyon,"
as, by making a verb out of the Spanish noun,
the people of the country describe the streams as
performing the feat of such rock passages, where
their banks are inapproachable, and trails or roads
are sent over or around; but this rock-guarded
career of the great river of the interior basin of
the Continent is the grand canyon of the world,
and one of its most wonderful marvels.   Its passage
in well protected boats by careful navigators can
scarcely be deemed impracticable, however dangerous, and the country will await the Powell movement through it with eager interest.

The whole field of observation and inquiry which
Professor Powell has undertaken is more interesting and important than any which lies before our
men of science.   The wonder is they have neglected it so long.   Here are seen the central forces
that formed the Continent; here more striking
studies in physical geography, geology, and natural
history, than are proffered anywhere else   New
knowledge and wide honors await those who cata-
logue and define them.   I can but think the inquiry, vast and important as it is, is fortunate in its

inquirer. Professor Powell is well educated, an en-
thusiast, resolute, a gallant leader, as his other title
of Major and an absent arm, won and lost in the
war, testify,—seemingly well-endowed physically
and mentally for the arduous work of both body
and brains that he has undertaken. He is every
way the soul, as he is the purse of the expedition;
he leads the way in all danger and difficulty, and
his wife, a true helpmeet, and the only woman with
the party, is the first to follow.

But while talking with the Professor, our reduced party has chosen a new leader,—General R.
F. Lord of Georgetown,—and is packed, bridled
and saddled for the start. We cross the river,
look gratefully and regretfully for the last time on
the Hot Springs, pass through the Indian encampment, and go lingering back over the long hill
that we had galloped down so gladly three days
before. Two-thirds the day's ride was the same
we had passed over in coming in; then we turned
to the left, the Boulder Mountain lying on the
opposite side of the lower end of the Park from
Berthoud; and soon we passed into a succession of
woods and open meadows, alternating with picturesque effects, as we gradually ascended the mountain, and offering fine views of sections of the Park
from occasional bluffs. The grass was thicker and
greener than in the more exposed parts of the Park;
the pines and firs and cotton-wood were in full variety and beauty; and the flowers grew gayer,—altogether it was a pleasanter country to ride leisurely
through than we had yet met with.

At the end of some twenty-five miles, we camped for the night, in the edge of the woods, fronting an open area of water-courses, grass and willows, with plenty of evidence that the beavers had a settlement there. An old bower of evergreens was cleared up and strengthened to lay our blankets under; and big fires kept off the cold of a ten thousand feet elevation, until three to four o'clock in the morning, when, by their subsidence and the increasing chill, everybody was in a shiver, and glad enough that an early call to morning duty soon summoned us up and astir. The water was freezing, and the grass and shrubs were stiff with frost, so stiff and yet so dry from lack of moisture in the air, that neither then, nor after the sun had softened them, was there wet to be won by walking among them. It was a perfectly dry freeze, and this is why these summer frosts do no more harm to vegetation, and delicate flowers thaw out and go on in their sweet short life in these high mountains.

The clouds gathered, and the rain-drops fell, as we finished breakfast and packed and saddled for the cold hard ride over the mountains. In an hour we were out of the timber, and a dreary waste of rock, relieved only by a thin grass at first, then by mosses, and always by flowers, lay before and all around us. The storm grew thick and fast, hail and snow; the trail wasted itself in the open area; the ground was being rapidly covered with the white snow; straggling was forbidden, and "close up" and "push on" were the orders from the front. The promised view of park and plains, of range on

on range, was lost; only thick, dark clouds, hanging
over impenetrable abysses, were around and below
us; the storm bit like wasps; beards gathered snow
and ice; the mules and horses winced under the
blasts,—it was a forlorn looking company for a
pleasure party.

But there was exhilaration in the unseasonable
struggle; there was something jolly in the idea of
thus confounding the almanacs, and finding February in August. At the summit of the Pass,—
thirteen thousand feet high,—the storm abated its
intensity to let us dismount and pick out of the
snow the little yellow flowers that crept up among
the rocks everywhere. Then it rolled over again,
and now with thunder and lightning, pealing and
flashing close around us. Here our laggard pack
mules with their drivers came hurrying up and forward; Charley Utter saying as he spurred them by
that perhaps we might like it, but for him "hell was
pleasanter and safer than a thunder-storm on the
range."   .

But as we descended the elements calmed; the
clouds opened visions of the new valleys, and flashes
of sunlight unveiled the great mysteries of the upper mountains. Summer was again around us; and
though it was hardly noon, the spot we had reached
was so rarely charming, and the sun so refreshing,
that we halted, loosed our animals, made our coffee,
lunched, and basked on the rocks in the sunshine
for a long, delightful hour. We were on a narrow
crest of the mountain, shooting out into the valley,
and not over twenty feet wide. On either side,

there was a sharp almost perpendicular descent for at least one thousand feet in one case, and seven hundred and fifty in the other. At the foot on our right were two lovely lakes, one almost an absolute circle, rock and grass bound, fed by great snow-banks between us and them, and feeding in turn the South Boulder Creek. On our left, a grassy slope, so steep that it was impossible to walk down except in long zigzags, and far away at the bottom among the trees ran the North Boulder from out the mountains. Everywhere about us, where the snow and the rocks left space, were the greenest of grass, the bluest of harebells, the reddest of paint-er's brush, the yellowest of sunflowers and butter-cups. All, with brightest of sun and bluest of sky, made up such a contrast to our morning ride that we were all in raptures with the various beauties of the scene, and feel still that no spot in all our travel is more sacred to beauty than this of our noon camp on Boulder.

But, as if to frame and fasten the picture still more strongly, we were hardly in the saddle again, before the storm set in anew, and we rode all the afternoon under snow or rain. There is what is called a road over into Middle Park by this Pass, and strong wagons with oxen or mules make the passage; but the difficulties they encounter are frightful,—mud and rocks, rivers and ravines,—it is hard to imagine how any wheels can surmount them and remain whole,—and few do. Our trail followed the road only in part; it made short cuts over hills, through woods, and across valleys, and

was full of variety, annoyance, sometimes of difficulty; but we found all less vexatious than the
descent of Berthoud Pass, and, following the South
Boulder Creek, came at last, wet and weary, into
the nearly deserted mining village of South Boulder.   Here we found welcome around the fire of
the post-office; a deserted cabin was thrown open
to us for our baggage and our meals; and a big
barn's loft with fresh hay furnished a magnificent
bedroom.   We dried, we ate, having fresh meat,
cream and vegetables added to our bill of fare, and
we slept, all in luxury.   Half the village was pre-
occupied by a large party of men and women, some
twenty to thirty, from the villages farther down the
valley, on their way into the Park by the road we
had come out.   They had ox teams for their baggage, saddle animals to carry themselves, and a cow
to furnish fresh milk; and thus generously equipped
were jollily entering upon camp life among the
mountains for ten days or a fortnight.

An early start the next morning, and a rapid gallop of ten miles over good roads, across the hills, by
scattered saw-mills, farm-houses, and mining-camps,
brought us into the valley of North Clear Creek, and
to the higgledy-piggledy but brisk town of Central City in season for the morning stage to Denver.
Our old friends here gave us hearty welcome, but
stared at our costumes in grim dismay, and some
took us for "honest miners" come to town from the
mountains for fresh supplies.   Here, too, the party
separated; the Vice-President going on to Denver
with some of the others; but the Governor (Bross)

and myself and our Georgetown friends, first eating
a French dinner by way of contrast to camp diet and
manners, rode on over another range of hills into
the South Clear Creek valley. And here, again, a
bath at the Idaho warm springs, and a couple of
days' rest and recreation at Mill City and Georgetown have prepared us for another and still more
select expedition into the highest mountain tops of
the country.

VII.

OVER GRAY'S PEAK TO SOUTH PARK.

A Private Outfit for a Grand Mountain Excursion—Gray's Peaks
and What They Showed Us—The Finest Mountain View in the
World—Saturday Night Camp in the Snake River Valley—
Sunday Travel with Commodore Decatur—A Butter Ranch—
How Life Goes in Camp, and What it Costs—The Blue River
Valley—Breckenridge, and over the Range into South Park
through Thunder and Lightning, Hail and Rain.

SOUTH PARK, Colorado, August, 1868.

WHILE the Vice-President, Governor Hunt, and
a considerable party of Denver friends were to
accompany our ladies into the South Park by the
usual wagon road from that point, Governor Bross,
General Lord and myself made a short cut but
rougher journey over two high ranges of mountains, much of the way impassable to vehicles, and
met them here. Our chief object was to ascend
Gray's Peaks, the highest summits yet accurately
measured in the Colorado mountains, and from
their central position commanding the widest and
most majestic views to be obtained in the country.
· Such a load as we put on our single pack mule: a
great overtopping cube of blankets and sacks of
meat and bread, and four little feet sticking out

beneath, were all that could be seen as it went shaking along on a mysterious trot. Sending the outfit and our outfitter, Ashley Franklin, by an easier path over to where we intended to camp for the night, we three started early Saturday morning from Georgetown,—distance fifteen miles to Gray's Peaks, and, by virtue of mines among the mountains, a good wagon road two-thirds the way. It was an object to get to the summit as early as possible, before afternoon haze or cloud should dim the view, and we galloped rapidly through aspen groves, then among larger pines, by the side of rapidly descending streams, around and around, up and up, and finally out above the trees, where grass and flowers had all life to themselves, and again above these and only thin mosses lived among the stones, and yet still higher, where the mountains became great walls of rock, or immense mounds of broken stone, as if they had been run through a crusher for the benefit of Mr. Macadam. Such was the character of Gray's Peaks. Great patches of snow divided place with the rocks, and fed the clear, cold rivulets that started out from every sheltered nook or side of the mountains; but they only added to the cold dreariness of the scene. The only life was grasshoppers,—here they were still by thousands, by millions, sporting in the air and frisking over the snow, but the latter's chill seemed soon to overcome their life, for they lay dead in countless numbers upon its white surface. In some places the dead grasshoppers could have been shoveled up by the bushels, and down at the edges of the snow cold grasshopper soup was to be had *ad libitum.* There was a feast here for the bears, but we could see none enjoying it.

Gray's Peaks,—great mounds or monuments of loose, broken stone,—shoot up sharply from a single base, in the midst of very high mountains all about. Their sharpness increases the appearance of the fact of their superior hight. Below, the two seem but a rifle shot apart; above, they are manifestly several miles away from each other; but their common paternity, their similarity in form, effect and views, entitle them to bear the common name. It was probably given originally to the lower peak alone by Dr. C. C. Parry of St. Louis, who has been, so far, the most thorough scientific explorer of the higher mountain regions of Colorado, and in honor of the distinguished Cambridge botanist, Professor Gray; but though there are persistent rivals for the name of the other and higher peak,—Dr. Parry himself, we believe, has suggested that of Professor Torrey for it,—the local judgment insists that they shall go together with the name of Gray. There are now trails for horses to the top of each,—that to the higher was nearly finished while we were there; and though the path to the lower is the more easy and familiar, our ambition was not content with anything less than the highest, and spite of fatigue and cold we struck out for it. Going through a snow-drift at least fifteen feet high, and coming out above all snow deposits, we fastened our animals with stones at the end of the path, and slowly toiled the remaining quarter

of a mile over the loose rocks,—the thin air oblig-
ing us to stop every three minutes to gain our
breath,—and at high noon sat upon the highest
peak of the highest known mountain of the great
Rocky Mountain range.   Dr. Parry made the lower
peak fourteen thousand two hundred and fifty-one
feet high; the highest must be at least fourteen
thousand five hundred.

The scene before us was ample recompense for
double the toil.   It was the great sight in all our
Colorado travel.   In impressiveness,—in overcom-
ingness, it takes rank with the three or four great
natural wonders of the world,—with Niagara Falls
from the Tower, with the Yosemite Valley from
Inspiration Point.   No Swiss mountain view carries such majestic sweep of distance, such sublime
combination of hight and breadth and depth; such
uplifting into the presence of God; such dwarfing
of the mortal sense, such welcome to the immortal
thought.   It was not beauty, it was sublimity; it
was not power, nor order, nor color, it was majesty;
it was not a part, it was the whole; it was not man
but God, that was about, before, in us.   Mountains
and mountains everywhere,—even the great Parks,
even the unending Plains seemed but patches among
the white ranges of hills stretching above and beyond one another.   We looked into Middle Park
below us on the north; over a single line of mountains into South Park, below us on the south,—but
beyond both were the unending peaks, the everlasting hills.   To the west, the broadest, noblest ranges
of mountains,—there seemed no breaks among them

except such as served to mark the end of one and the beginning of another, and no possible limit to their extension. The snow whitened all, covered many, and brought out their lines in conspicuous majesty. Over one óf the largest and finest, the snow-fields lay in the form of an immense cross, and by this it is known in all the mountain views of the territory. It is as if God has set His sign, His seal, His promise there,—a beacon upon the very center and hight of the Continent to all its people and all its generations. Beyond this up-lifted what seemed to be the only mountain in all the range of view higher than the peak upon which we stood. It is named Sopris Peak upon some of the maps, but has never been explored, and is more completely covered with snow than any other.

Turning to the east we find relief in the softer and yet majestic and unending vision of the Plains, —on, on they stretch in everlasting green and gray until lost in the dim haze that is just beginning to rise along the horizon. Directly below us, great rough seams in the mountain sides, as if fire and water had been at work for ages to waste and overturn; dreary areas of red and brown and gray rocks; masses of timber; bits of green in the far-down valley; flashes of darkness where little lakes nestled amid the rocks, fed by snow, and feeding the streams,—Nature everywhere in her original forms, and her abounding waste of wealth, as if here was the great supply store and workshop of Creation, the fountain of Earth. Looking from side to side, above, below, and around,—impressed,

oppressed everywhere with the presence of the Beginning; it was almost unconsciously and instinct-
ively that we turned again and at last, as Mrs. Browning makes Romney Leigh, "toward the east:"—

> "————where faint and fair,
> Along the tingling desert of the sky,
> Beyond the circle of the conscious hills,
> Were laid in jasper-stone as clear as glass
> The first foundations of that new, near Day,
> Which should be builded out of heaven, to God."

It was difficult to leave this citadel of earth, this
outpost of heaven; but our time and our strength
were both exhausted. The long gallop, the hard
climb, more, the excitement of the vision of earth
and sky at this elevation of over fourteen thousand
feet above the ocean level had used up our nerve-
power; the cool breezes, too, chilled us; and after
lunching, we regained our horses, and pushed down
the other side of the mountain from that we came up.

There was only a dim trail to follow, running
hither and thither around and among the hills, and
then across and along the valleys of the streams that
came in from every mountain crevice and snow-
bank. We crossed Colfax Park, a little gem of grass
and flowers, with Colfax Lake at its head, a great
rock bowl of clear water, high in the hill-side, and
pouring its surplus over a sharp natural wall of
stone,—so named by an enthusiastic and appreciative miner in the lower valley, who would hardly be
reconciled with us that we had not brought the
Vice-President to witness how happily and fitly he
had been honored here. We passed also through

many a beaver village; but the inhabitants gave us
no visible welcome; they modestly let their works
speak for them. The woods grew thick and mel-
low; the aspen tender, the spruces silver-hung and
silver-tongued; and we came at last,—a long ten
miles from the summit of Gray's Peak,—to our
proposed camping spot, the junction of two forks
of the Snake River and of the two trails from
Georgetown.

Here, the grass was abundant, the stream ran pure
and strong, unpolluted by miner's mud, fuel was
plenty, even the mosquitoes sang a welcome, but
no Ashley Franklin, no pack-mule was to be seen,
no blankets, no food, no nothing, that belonged to
us, but weariness and hunger. We sounded the
war-whoop of the country,—a shrill, far-reaching
cry; and back the voices came, not only from our
lagging outfit, but from miners here and there among
the hills, just finishing their day's work, and wondering who had come into their wilderness now.
The mules took up the refrain, and bellowed from
"depths that overflow" their welcome to each other.
Soon we were at home, the coffee brewing, the ham
stewing, and a hole through the peach can; Commodore Decatur, the prince of prospectors, the character of all Colorado characters, dropped in·to bid
us welcome to his principality, on his way from mine
to cabin; under the frosts of night and the smoke
of the camp fire, the merry mosquitoes flew away;
our tent was raised, our blankets spread; and the
peace of Saturday night and a day richly spent
reigned over us four and no more.

But camp life is not all comfort. This very blessed Saturday night on the Snake River, the wind took turns in coming out of the three or four valleys that converged upon our camping-ground, and blew the virulent smoke in upon us. Shift the fire, change the blanket, still the smoke followed us, as if charmed, and was discomfort and sleeplessness to all, poison to at least one. There was a yearning for something delicate for the Sunday morning breakfast,—a bit of cream toast, or a soft egg, and some milk-ameliorated coffee; but the knurly little "Jack," that carried our "bed and board," had no provision for sensitive stomachs, and we had to take our victual and drink "straight," —plain ham and bread and butter and black coffee,—or go without. But that best and cheapest of doctors and nurses, the sun came to our relief; and later in the day a pitcher of butter-milk completed and capped his healing triumphs. Mr. Richardson records my sarcastic contempt for buttermilk three years ago, but I take it all back now,—no cup of it shall ever pass from my lips again other than empty. It comes to a faint and forlorn stomach like woman's sympathy to a bruised heart.

Governor Bross galloped back into the hills to make a call at a solitary cabin half a dozen miles away; Commodore Decatur dropped in with the Lord's blessing on his lips, and picked me up for a ride down the river,—whither we were bound;— General Lord followed along with his fishing-pole, lingering over the streams; and the mule and his master strolled more leisurely after, to protect the

rear and gather in the Governor. There was a
rough wagon road most of the way, chiefly through
woods, occasionally across an open park, frequently
over or in the stream, but the hills kept close guard,
and the eye was not allowed to wander far away for
beauty. But the "Commodore," who, to thirty years
of schools and civilization, has added twenty of border life in Mexico, in Nebraska and in Colorado, living at times among the Indians, and for many a
season in his solitary cabin in these elevated valleys,
kept me entertained with his original experiences,
his keen observations on men and manners, and his
quaint yet rich philosophies. He is an old Greek
philosopher,—with an American variation; as wise
as Socrates, as enthusiastic as a child, as mysterious in life and purpose as William H. Seward or
an Egyptian sphynx, as religious as a Methodist
class-leader,—he ranks high among the individual
institutions and idiosyncracies of Colorado, such as
Governor Hunt, Editor Goldrick and Charley Utter, whom not to know is to miss the next piquant
things to its Mountains and Parks.

We sauntered thus through ten miles in four
hours, gathering up at last the stragglers in the
rear, and came out then into a grand opening in
the valley. The timber disappeared; the hills
sharpened into a dead wall on one side, and swept
away in soft rolling outlines on the other; a wide
stretch of intervale lay between, while pretty groves
of trees tempered the distant knolls and broke the
abruptness of forests beyond. We were again,
indeed, in Middle Park, though a high range of

mountains and a long, hard ride separated us from that part of it which we visited the week before.

Away under a bluff, a speck in the distance, was a log-cabin,—"the Georgia Ranch," towards which we now rode with freshened speed. Here in a cabin of two rooms, with a log milk-house outside, the only dwellers in this rich pasture park, were a man, his wife and daughter; their home and farm were in Southern Colorado, but they had come up here in the spring with forty or fifty cows, and were making one hundred and forty-five pounds of butter a week, and selling it to the miners in the cabins and camps among the hills ten to fifteen miles around, for seventy-five cents a pound; when the snows begin to fall in October, they will drive the herd back to their southern pastures,—the increase of the cows will pay all expenses, and the one hundred dollars a week or more cash for butter and milk, is clear profit. The dairy cabin was a "sight to behold," such piles of fresh golden butter, such shelves of full pans of milk,—there wasn't room for another pound or pan; and yet the demand far exceeds the supply,—it was a favor to be allowed to purchase the treasures of "Georgia Ranch." It was our "Commodore's" Sunday diversion to ride down these dozen miles, fill his weekly butter-pail and his milk-can, and gallop back in season for a Sunday night supper with his cabin comrade of "mush and milk."

These mining hermits in the mountains manage to live well,—they become adepts in cooking; with flour and meal and fresh meat, potatoes and onions,

dried and canned fruits, the bill of fare is appetizing;
and the cost of the "best tables" is from seventy-five
cents to one dollar a day.   Nor are they always thus
exiles from society; their season in the hills, hunting new lodes or developing old ones, is confined
to the summer; when cold and snow come, they
flee to the villages or to Denver,—to live as leisurely and luxuriously as what they have made the
past season or hope to make the next will permit.

We "packed" a bottle of cream, filled our water
canteen with milk, took Decatur's Methodistic ben-
ediction,—"May the Lord take a liking to you,"—
with a hearty "amen," and rode down the valley,
by numerous soda and other mineral springs, three
or four miles farther, to our camp for the night.
This was at a still more picturesque spot,—a trinity
of rivers, a triangle of mountains.   The Blue and
the Snake Rivers and Ten Mile Creek all meet and
mingle here within a few rods; each a strong, hearty
stream, from its own independent circle of mountains; and while the waters unresisting swam together, the hills stood apart and away, frowning in
dark forests and black rock, and cold with great
snow-fields, overlooking the scene, which green
meadows, and blue sky, and warm sun mellowed
and brightened.   A neck of land, holding abundant grass and fuel, between the three rivers at the
point of junction, offered a magnificent camping-
ground.   It is a spot to settle down upon and keep
house at for a week.   Ten Mile Creek overflows
with trout; General Lord took ten pounds out of a
single hole in a less number of minutes,—a single fish

weighing about three pounds; and deer and game birds must be readily findable in the neighborhood. The Blue isn't blue,—its waters have been troubled by the miners, and it gives its name and mud color to the combined stream, which flows off through an open, inviting valley to join the Grand, and thence to make up the grand Colorado of the West.

We had a lesson in precaution, after unloading, and proceeding to make camp here, by finding that nobody had any matches; we could not shoot flame out of our metallic-cartridge pistols; nor had we the Indian accomplishment of rubbing fire out of two sticks; so the best mule was put over the road to the "Ranch" and back at a very un-mule-like-gait, to bring us the means of kindling our camp fire. But we had a sumptuous supper, of cream toast and trout, with milk for our coffee, and a sweet night in camp, though lulled to sleep by the roll of thunder and the patter of a brisk shower, with high wind and sharp lightning; and we turned reluctantly up the valley of the Blue, the next morning, with the resolution to come to stay at this point another season.

We had come this way through a little obstinacy of our own, instead of taking the common and short cut over the hills, from the valley of the upper Snake to Breckenridge,—sure that the conjunction of the Blue, the Snake and Ten Mile must offer something worth seeing in the way of valley and mountain scenery; and so we were quite proud of our gener-ous repayment, and desire all future travelers to make a note of our route, and follow it. The valley of the Blue, both above and below where we

struck it, is altogether one of the most interesting
scenic sections of the territory; it should be taken
in going into or out from the Hot Springs; there
is no route so rich in interest and beauty as that
through it from the Middle to the South Park, or
vice versa, or from Georgetown over Gray's Peaks
into either Park,—and we were sorry not to have
time for wider exploration of its lines.

Our day's ride now followed up the river to its
very head in the mountains. The first eight miles
was through a fine open grazing country, and we
found a magnificent herd of fat cattle, strongly
marked with Durham blood, enjoying its rich
grasses. They had been sent up here to fatten
for the summer from some of the ranches of the
lower valleys, and, perhaps, to furnish fresh beef to
the mining camps, which are quite numerous among
the side valleys of the neighborhood. Nearly all
our day's ride we were in sight of the ditches that
had been built to carry water to the rich beds of
sand that were in course of being washed over for
gold deposits at various localities in the valleys.
One of these ditches is twelve miles long; tapping
the Blue away up in the mountains, it takes a vigorous stream along and around the mountain sides,
up and down, from gulch to gulch, parting with
portions at different points on the route to little
companies of miners at so much per foot; and, de-
ployed into sand-banks, swept through long boxes,
tarried in screens and by petty dams, it does its
work of separating the tiny particles of gold from the
earth, and finds its way back to the parent stream,

miles from where it left it, but bringing the pollutions of the world and of labor with it. Many thousands of dollars are invested in these ditches; sometimes they are made and owned by individuals, who also work the mines or deposits of gold to which they lead, but oftener now they belong to companies that have no other interest than to sell water from them to those who mine alone. Generally they have passed out of the hands of their builders, who rarely realized anything but expectations, vast and vain, from them.

At Breckenridge we got above the washings, and the river was clear again. This is the center of these upper mining interests, but a village of only twenty or thirty cabins, located ten thousand feet high, and scarcely habitable in winter, though many of the miners do hibernate here through the season of snow and cold that begins in early October and ends in June. There is a good hotel here, of logs to be sure, with a broad buxom matron, and black-eyed beauties of daughters, to whom, after dinner, we consigned Governor Bross, with warning against his fascinations, while General Lord and myself, with our guide, went on over the range into the South Park. The miners were to be gathered in the next night for speeches from the Vice-President and the Governor, and the latter awaited the occasion and the former's arrival.

There was a good wagon road all our way, leading from Breckenridge to the summit of Breckenridge Pass, through open woods, flower-endowed meadows, a broken, various and interesting moun-

5*

tain country, often giving majestic views of the higher and snow-crowned peaks, with glimpses of valleys and parks below and beyond. The Pass is just above the timber line, about twelve thousand feet high, and as we mounted it, a cold storm gathered upon the snow-fields above us, wheeled from peak to peak in densely black clouds, and soon broke in gusts of wind, in vivid lightning, in startlingly close and loud claps of thunder, in driving snow, in pelting hail, in drizzling rain. We were below the storm's fountain, but near enough to see all its grand movements, to feel its awful presence, to be shaken with fear, to gather inspiration. The rapidity of its passage from side to side, from peak to peak, was wonderful; the crashing loudness of its thunderous discharges awful; one moment we felt like "fleeing before the Lord," the next charmed and awed into rest in His presence.

But it was dreary enough, when the thundering and the flashing ceased, and the clouds stopped their majestic movement, and hung in deep mists over all the mountains and the valleys, and the rain poured ceaselessly down. The poetry was gone, and gathering overcoats and rubber closely about us, we bent our heads to the undeviating shower, and pushed gloomily and ghastily on. It seemed a long ride down mountain side and through valley to Hamilton,—woods that made us feel even more pitiful; open valleys that made the rain more pitiless; streams twisted out of place and shape by ruthless miners ; desolated cabins, doorless, windowless,—even the storm was more inviting ; Tarryall, where thousands dug and washed sands for gold three and four years ago, and now only two or three cabins, mud-patched and turf-warmed, sent forth the smoke of home; a solitary dirt-washer trudging along from his day's mountain work, with dinner-pail and pickax,—out at last, where, through the opening mists, we could see the long, level reaches of South Park, and into Hamilton,—fifty or more vacant or decaying cabins and two log hotels,—where one thousand men mined in '60 to '64, and gayety and vice reigned, and now a dozen or twenty men and three or four women were the entire population; a grimy, dirty looking village of the past, for all the world in the storm like an old Swiss mountain village, with manure heaps in front of the houses, and a few sorry looking horses and mules scattered about the pastures.

It was a comfortless promise after so comfortless a ride. We passed on by the village to a plateau above the river, and tried to make camp; but everything was wet,—the water especially so and very muddy; we couldn't start a fire; our guide was obstinate for going to the hotel, and after long struggling against it, we capitulated and went. We gained shelter and warmth, and a good supper, and chapters of country experiences around the fire with the tobacco, and a small bed for two; but there are more real comfort and better air and greater cleanliness and real independence in camp than in these pent-up mountain inns. It was hard to accept such compromise with civilization after the luxuries we had enjoyed in our ground and tent homes.

VIII.

THE SOUTH PARK AND MOUNT LINCOLN.

Sunshine and Reunion in the South Park—The Beauties of the Park—Camping Experiences—The Ascent of Mount Lincoln, the Mother of the Mother Mountains—A Snow Storm on the Summit—Montgomery and Fairplay—The Everlasting Plattes— Over the Range again into the Arkansas Valley.

UPPER ARKANSAS VALLEY, August, 1868.

WITH the morning at Hamilton came sunshine and beautiful views of the South Park country, that lay spread out before us in unending stretches of green prairie; here lifted up by a perfect embankment to a new level and going on again in another plain; there rolling off into hills with patches of evergreen; now bringing down from the mountains, still through pastures green, tributaries to the main river; offering on every hand glimpses of beckoning repetitions of itself through and over hills; while all around in the distant horizon huge mountains stood sentinel, guarding this great upper garden-spot of the territory, as if jealous lest its frontiers be invaded, its lands despoiled. No so fine a combination of the grand beauty of the plains, of the lovely beauty of the hills, of the majestic beauty of the mountains ever spread itself before my eyes. Water-courses were abundant, groves and forests were placed with sufficient frequency to diversify the scene and relieve and kindle the eye, while mountains, near and remote, gave their impressive sanction and completeness to the picture. The coloring was brighter yet softer than in Middle Park; and we felt that Colorado had indeed reserved her choicest landscape treasures for us to the last.

Before noon, six miles away, we caught sight of our companions from Denver, coming over the hill, —some on horseback, some in light carriages, and the rest in wagons with the baggage. They looked like one of the patriarchal families of Old Testament times, sons and daughters, servants and asses, moving from one country to another, in obedience to high commandment; and as if representatives of another tribe, we rode out to greet and welcome them to our goodly land. We propitiated their stomachs with our treasured big trout; and after lunch upon the open prairie, the grand caravan moved on, in somewhat disorderly array.

We made a dozen miles, along the northern line of the Park, over a rich, rolling country, starred by occasional lakes, darkened by frequent forests, shadowed by the everlasting snow fields of the mountains. The inevitable afternoon storm came upon us midway, and we rode into Fairplay, the most considerable town of the South Park country, variously wet and considerably disgusted. The ladies stopped by the hospitable fires of the village, while the men went on, and made camp on a hill overlooking the valley, shaded by a few old and stunted pines, and circled by a miner's ditch full of furiously running water.   Here half a dozen fires were kindled, as many tents stretched, and, the storm passing away, everybody came into camp, and sleep followed supper to the satisfaction of all.

We moved but a dozen miles the next day, up into the mountains more closely, and near Montgomery, from whence some of us were to ascend Mount Lincoln the day after.   These winding valleys, leading out from the Park proper to the mountains, are very beautiful, and the road between Fairplay and Montgomery, which lies close under the highest mountains, offers a succession of brilliantly picturesque mountain and valley views.   The valleys are broad, and fertile with green grass, and bright with flowers, and broken with forest patches, while the mountains rise all about in every attitude, and reach up on every hand to snow-fields, flashing in the morning and reddening in the evening sun.

Our camp was a gay one that night,—it lay scattered along a green hill-side, a few rods from a river, and directly under a forest; fuel was abundant, and the fires burned bright and high in all directions; we were not worn with the day's travel; anticipation of the mountain excursion the next morning, was keen and exhilarating; and song and speech and dance around the central camp fire exhausted the hours till bed-time.

It was a happy thought to call the parent mountain of this region, of the whole Rocky Mountain range proper, for the President who guided the

Nation so proudly through civil war and slavery to peace and freedom. Peer among presidents and mother among mountains is LINCOLN. The higher Gray's Peak is as high, possibly a hundred or two feet higher; but Mount Lincoln is broader, more majestic, more mountainous. Out from its wide-spreading folds stretch three or four lines of snow-covered mountains; within its recesses spring the waters of three great rivers, the Platte, the Arkansas and the Colorado, that fertilize the plains of half the Continent, and bury themselves, at last, two in the Atlantic and the third in the Pacific Ocean. This is the initial point in our geography, and a fountain-head of national wealth and strength. This geographical parentage, the representative association of its name and office, and the enthusiasm kindled by our accounts of the view from Gray's Peak, spread a zest among our party for climbing Mount Lincoln; and though the morning was strewn with showers, and huge black clouds hung over the mountain tops in alternation with great rifts of sunshine, these revealing fresh-fallen fields of snow, we determined to take our chances, and galloped off, a dozen strong, women and men, up the valley to Montgomery.

The rain poured relentlessly through these five miles; but then the sunshine came out, and joined by half a dozen more at that point, we turned directly up the mountain side. For two or three miles there is a rough wagon road; beyond that not even a trail that is fixed. Catching sight of the distant goal, we scattered irregularly over the

intervening slopes and ravines; first through richest grasses and most abundant and high-colored
flowers; then across huge snow-fields, so soft under the summer sun, that our animals could not
bear us without floundering in dangerous depths,
and we had to dismount and walk and lead; next
over wide but steep fields of thin mosses, delicate
in leaf and blossom to the last degree, pink and
white and blue,—the very final condensed expression of nature; all beauty, all tenderness, all sweet-
ness in essence; and at last, beyond all growth,
beyond all snow, out upon miles of broken stones,
immeasurably deep, as steep as they could lie.

To ascend over these was tough work; the wind
blew biting cold; clouds charged with hail and
snow every few minutes swept over, through us;
the air was so rare that the animals labored for
breath at every step; the sides so steep and the
stones so loose as to render the footing fickle,
even dangerous; we could only make upward progress in slow degree by long, zigzag courses back
and forth; and every few minutes the panting,
trembling horses and mules would come to a stubborn stop in very fear of their footing. Then we
had to dismount and reassure them by leading the
way, or find firmer paths. But at last we got as
far as horses could go; and a climb of five hundred
feet remained for ourselves of even steeper and still
loose-lying rocks to the summit. Then we found
our hearts and lungs, if never before; work as fast
as they could, shaking our very frames in the haste
to keep up with their duty, we still had to stop and

rest every thirty or forty feet, and let them get even with the air.

Finally on the very crest of the mammoth mountain, the one spot higher than all others, than all around so far as could be seen. Our hopes our fears belied, our fears our hopes in turn; the sweep of the horizon was broken by thick clouds; and we could not compare the view with its rival, from Gray's Peak; but the contending elements lent a new majesty, almost a terror to the scene. Sunshine and storm were continually at war; clouds and clearness constantly changing places; now it was all light to the east, and Gray's Peak and all the intervening mountains to the Plains, the Plains themselves, Denver itself glowed in golden sunshine, while in the west everything was shrouded in blackness and despair; then the clouds came upon and over us, pelting us with snow, and passing by opened great lines of brightness to the west, and we could see on to indefinable distances of snow-covered mountains,—Sopris Peak, the mountain with the snow cross, a continent of rocks and snow, dreary yet beautiful in color, majestic yet fascinating in form. So we caught long narrow glimpses of the South Park, and the Arkansas valley, south of us; and Pike's Peak in one direction and Long's Peak in another were not denied us,—sentinels of nature in the far off corners of the territory, rising above clouds, over intervening storms; while deep chasms, yawning recesses opened in ghastliness through the clouds below us on every side.

The whole vision, fickle, forbidding in many features, always surprising, never satisfying, piqueing us by what was withheld, astonishing us by what was given, though disappointing our hopes, yet was vastly finer than our fears. It was the wildest of mountain views and mountain experiences, such as may be welcomed as a variety, though not chosen as the reward for a single excursion. Similar experiences in the high Alps are tamer every way; there is less variety in the landscape; less color in the mountains and the atmosphere; above all, less sweep of distance, less piling of mountain on mountain, through the long openings in the clouds.

We waited as long as the freezing air and the driving snow would let us for wider views of earth and sky; but clouds and storm growing denser, and having finished our lunch of sandwiches and sardines, pickles and peaches, and, coffee being out of the question, a necessary flask of whisky, we retraced the tedious, hard-going way to the valley. Far up, where only rocks reigned, beautiful white and blue birds, like large doves, but called mountain partridges, trotted or flew tamely about us; and a revolver sadly repaid the faith of some of them. Back among the flowers, we gathered large bouquets of bright painter's brush, harebells, fringed gentians, lupins and quaint grasses, and rode into Montgomery aglow with color and excitement, and wet alike from perspiration, snow and rain.

The whole excursion up from and back to Montgomery occupied five hours. The distance cannot be more than six miles to the top; and the hight of the mountain, though never exactly measured, must exceed fourteen thousand feet above the sea level. The wildest estimates are made by the local population of these higher peaks of Colorado; but unless it be Sopris Peak in the far West, it is not probable that any one of them rises as high as Mount Whitney in the Sierra Nevada of California, which is known to be above fifteen thousand feet. Gray, Lincoln, Pike's and Long's Peaks are the four great mountains of explored Colorado; they are all above fourteen thousand feet high, but probably no one goes higher than fourteen thousand five hundred.

Montgomery, which lies close at the foot of Mount Lincoln, on the inside, and is about ten thousand feet high, is another of the deserted mining towns of Colorado. There are a hundred or two houses standing, but only one now occupied. Several years ago, the mines in the hill-sides were rich and remunerative, and a population of two or three thousand were gathered there. There was an operá house, and saloons and stores by the dozens; but the more readily worked ore gave out, there were no means to reduce profitably what followed in the mines, and fresher discoveries elsewhere invited the people "to move on." "Buckskin Joe" is another similar town, five miles off, under another spur of Mount Lincoln. There are good and rich mines at both places, and new ones are even still being discovered; but like most of the ores of Colorado, they await cheaper labor and simpler and more searching processes of treatment for their profitable use.

The solitary family in Montgomery, cultivated, tasteful people, such as we find everywhere among these mountain recesses, gave us a rich hospitality, —which means a "square meal" and a hearty welcome,—and, sunshine being now permanently the victor, we had a pleasant afternoon ride down the valley, by our now deserted camp of the night before, along the clear-running juices of old Lincoln, winding about among her child-hills, their snow-tops reddening under the descending sun, and giving depth and richness to the verdure of valley and forest.   Reaching Fairplay at dusk, we found the rest of the party,—those who did not go up Mount Lincoln,—had gone ten miles farther on, with tents, bag and baggage, and left us to the miserable resource of a night's life in town.   But the long-stretching log hotel and the country habit of close-packing,—no house is ever full here, so long as any bed has less than four in it, or there is a vacant corner to lay a blanket,— made accommodations for us all, even though the village was unusually crowded that night by reason of Mr. Colfax and Governor Bross stopping over to make speeches. But we missed the better victual, the wider space, the purer air of camp, and duly anathematized Governor Hunt and his various "little Indians," for running away from us.

The Platte River divides, subdivides, and redivides almost indefinitely; and when we get up here among its head waters, the brain fairly grows confused with the number of its forks or branches. The same name extends to the remotest subdivision; and we have the north branch of the south fork of the South Platte; and the middle fork of the north branch of the south fork of the South Platte, and so on *ad infinitum*. I wish the Coloradians would abolish the sinuosities and multiplications, and put the Plattes into numerals, as Platte 1, 2, 3, 4, 5, and so on. I verily believe they would run up to the hundreds; but that would be better than the "Peter Piper picked a peck of pickled peppers" nomenclature. Perhaps, though, they mean to make their geography take the place of classics as a discipline for the youthful mind; if so, they have hit upon a very ingenious substitute, not to say improvement. As between learning the Plattes and conjugating a Greek verb, where's the choice for hardness? All the time we were in the South Park, we were among Plattes, and getting to the heads of Plattes, and each was big enough and independent enough to go alone, and to deserve a name to itself. Fairplay lies on the Platte, and so did every one of our camping grounds for a week.

I believe I have exhausted my adjectives and every known variety of picture frame in trying to set the South Park landscapes in the mind's eye of the reader. But their soft coloring, their rich variety of outline, their long sweep of distance, their greyish-green grasses, their deep-green evergreens, their silvery-green aspens, their summer pictures in their winter frames,—here August, there rising around always January,—only seeing can be feeling and believing. Especially beautiful and exhilarating to sense and spirit are the approaches to

the mountains out from the central basin or prairie.
First, over slight and soft-rolling hills, through wide
valleys, around spurs of the mountains into new
valleys, each succeeding one narrower, finally into
canyons or chasms, and then up the abrupt hill-
side; flowers that had deserted the plains now
beginning, then trees ceasing, and snow-banks appearing; and finally catching the cold western
wind as it sweeps over the crest of pass or hill.
Occasionally, in the open prairie country, a ranch
where some successor of David tends his flocks;
in the narrow valleys, or on the hill-sides, the deserted cabins of gold-hunters, who had passed on;
every six or eight miles a new Platte to cross; and
at each ascended mountain-top the beginning of a
new Platte, running through tender grass out of a
little round lake, or oozing from under a huge
snow-bank.

These were our observations the next day, as
we galloped savagely on after the head-quarters of
the camp. We surprised it at lunch by our rapidity, and then all pushed on "over the range"
that divides South Park from the Arkansas valley. The South Park country is free from rocks
or stones; the waste of the mountains is broken
and pulverized before it reaches the valleys; and
even when we mount above grass and trees and
earth, the "rock-ribbed hills" are simply great deposits of small stones, or, more correctly, broken
rocks. This is one great element in the softness
of its scenery. But as we go over the mountains
into the Arkansas valley, there is a change; the

roads become rough with stones; boulders lie along the path or in the hill-sides, and the water-courses have thrust themselves through high walls of solid rock. There is more ruggedness and coarseness in nature; and while the want of it was not felt, now we welcome the new materials in the landscape. Our heavy baggage teams were slow in working up the huge hills and down, and we went into camp at the first passable widening of the side valley.

IX.

AN INDIAN SCARE—THE TWIN LAKES.

Alarming Indian Reports—The Savages on our Track—Scenes and
Thoughts in Camp—A Nervous Night and its Sufferings—The
Indian Question Generally—The Old False, the New True
Policy—The Relief of the Next Morning—The Arkansas Val-
ley and its Greetings—The Twin Lakes and their Beauties—
Sunday and Short-Cake—Taylor and Trout.

TWIN LAKES, Upper Arkansas Valley, September, 1868.

THE circle of our Colorado and border travel experience has been made complete by an Indian
scare. We have shared the horrible excitement of
the settlers, when the hostile Indians put on their
war-paint, raise their war-whoop, and dash wildly
upon the life and property of the whites. Just as
we were going into camp,—weary with mountain
travel, and our heaviest teams far behind,—this side
the range, there dashed in, on a gaunt white horse,
a grim messenger from Denver, with official advices
to Governor Hunt that the Indians of the Plains,
—the Cheyennes, Arapahoes and Sioux,—were on
the "war-path;" that from seeming friends they
had suddenly turned again to open foes; and were
raiding furiously all among the settlements, east,
north and south of Denver, stealing horses and

shooting the people. We were besought to keep among the mountains,—the homes of the friendly Utes,—as the only place of safety, for our company of territorial and federal officials would be a tempting prize for the red men; but the messenger, who proved to be a villainous sensationist,—though of course we did not know this then,—added to his written reports the alarming story that he had met the hostile Indians in the mountains, only that very day, that they had pursued and shot at him,—the rascal even showing as proof the bullet-holes in his saddle,—that he barely escaped by rapid riding, and that they were probably but a few miles back, and on our path.

Here was serious business, indeed, for such a party; burdened with overloaded wagons, tired horses and defenceless women and children; and all on pleasure and not on war intent. Messengers were sent back to hasten to camp all stragglers, and to warn the Indian agent, with his load of goods and rifles in the Park, to be on his guard, and to come forward. The secret could be kept from no one; the confusion and the excitement quickly grew intense; and that peculiar recklessness or indifference as to ordinary matters, that follows the presence of a deep emotion, was singularly manifest. Tents were shabbily put up; camp was disorderly made; supper was eaten in that mechanical, forced way, without regard to quantity, quality or clean plates, that happens when death is in the house; and elaborate toilets were dispensed with. But we huddled close in together; the animals were picketed near at hand; our fire-arms were put in good order; and up and down the road, trusty sentinels were posted. On each side were high abrupt hills; it was a "lovely spot" for an ambuscade; but the nearest anybody came to being killed was when one of our sentinels, during the midnight blackness of storm, suddenly entered upon the ground of the other. Indian-shod in sandals, and moving with that noiseless, stealthy tread that hunters unconsciously adopt, the one was almost upon the other before the latter discovered a foreign presence. There was a sudden click of the rifle's cock, a peremptory demand for "personal explanation" without delay, and then,—a friendly instead of a deadly greeting.

But it was a night to remember, with a shiver, —lying down in that far-off wilderness with the reasonable belief that before morning there was an even chance of an attack of hostile Indians upon our camp, more than half of whose numbers were women and children,—after an evening spent in discussing the tender ways Indians had with their captives, illustrated from the personal knowledge of many present; aroused after the first hour's feverish rest by a new messenger from another quarter, galloping into camp, and shouting, as if we were likely to forget, that "the Indians were loose, and hell was to pay;" followed by the coming of furious storm of rain and hail and thunder and lightning, sucking under our tents, beating through them, to wet pillows and blankets,—at any other time a dire grievance, now hardly an added trial; every ear stretched for unaccustomed sound, every heart beating anxiously, but every lip silent; all eagerly awaiting the slow-coming morning to bring renewal of life and the opportunity to go farther on and to safer retreats. To confess the unprosaic individual fact,—while I report the general truth,—this deponent had the soundest, sweetest night's sleep he had had in the mountains. Some natures will be perverse, and if one must be nervous, it is a great help to be conscious of it.

The experience brought serious thought to us all of the whole Indian question, that puzzle to Congress and eastern public opinion generally. And the failure, which this unexpected outbreak brings to the last and most promising experiment with the so-called but miscalled "peace policy," will probably lead to a more intelligent study and understanding of the whole subject by the country, and in the end to a resolute reformation of our past treatment of it. The truth here, as in many another dispute, lies between the two extremes of opinion and policy. The wild clamor of the border population for· the indiscriminate extermination of the savages, as of wolves or other wild beasts and vermin, is as unintelligent and barbarous, as the long dominant thought of the East against the use of force, and its incident policy of treating the Indians as of equal responsibility and intelligence with the whites, are unphilosophical and impracticable. The conflict between these two theories, with the varying supremacy of each, has brought us nothing but disaster and disgrace; we have alternately treated these vagrant children of the wilderness as if we were worse barbarians than themselves or downright fools. It is time we respected ourselves and commanded their respect. Now we do neither.

In the first place, the care of the Indians should be put into a single department at Washington. Its division between the war and interior secretaries is the cause of half our woes. The war office, as representing force, which is the first element in any successful dealing with ignorance and dependence, should monopolize their care. Then we should stop making treaties with tribes, cease putting them on a par with ourselves. We know they are not our equals; we know that our right to the soil, as a race capable of its superior improvement, is above theirs; and let us act openly and directly our faith. The earth is the Lord's; it is given by Him to the Saints for its improvement and development; and we are the Saints. This old Puritan premise and conclusion are the faith and practice of our people; let us hesitate no longer to avow it and act it to the Indian. Let us say to him, you are our ward, our child, the victim of our destiny, ours to displace, ours also to protect. We want your hunting-grounds to dig gold from, to raise grain on, and you must "move on." Here is a home for you, more limited than you have had; hither you must go, here you must stay; in place of your game, we will give you horses, cattle and sheep and grain; do what you can to multiply them and support yourselves; for the rest, it is our business to keep you from starving. You must not leave this home we have assigned you; the white man must not come hither; we will keep you in and him out; when the march of our empire demands this reservation of yours, we will assign you another; but so long as we choose, this is your home, your prison, your play-ground.

Say and act all this as if we meant it, and mean it. If the tribes would go and submit peaceably, well and good; if they would not, use the force necessary to make them. Treat them just as a father would treat an ignorant, undeveloped child. If necessary to punish, punish; subject any way; and then use the kindness and consideration that are consistent with the circumstances. Use the best of these white men of the border, these Indian agents, many of whom are most capable and intelligent and useful men, to carry out and maintain this policy, so far as is possible; use the army so far as is necessary to enforce it, but withhold the soldiers whenever it is not,—for their presence on an Indian reservation is demoralizing to both parties,—but let all authority proceed from a single head, and that head represent a single force.

Above all, stop the treaty-making humbug. It is the direct parent of all our Indian woes and theirs too. Neither party keeps the bargain. The Indian is cheated; the Senate changes the provisions; a quiddling secretary of the interior or Indian commissioner refuses to carry it out; and from secretary down through contractors and agents, something is taken off the promise to the ear by each, till it is thoroughly broken to the hope of the poor savage.

What the Indian wants is to be fed and clothed;
the treaty and those who fulfil it on our part may
or may not do this for him, oftenest not; he cannot tell what or how much he wants beforehand for
these ends, and if he did, and bargained for it, the
chances are ten to one that he fails to get it; or
getting it, squanders it at once, and now, hungry
and naked, he goes forth to seek relief by the simplest law of nature; and hence his excuse and the
excuse of his white sympathizers for war.

But establish Force for Bargain; Responsibility
for Equality; Parentage for Antagonism; see that
he is put apart and kept apart from the tide of
settlement and civilization; that he has food and
clothing, not in gross, but in detail; supplying
him the means to help himself in the simplest
forms possible,—stock raising is practicable to all
the tribes, and tilling the soil possible to most,—
and furnishing the rest from day to day; add such
education as he will take, such elevation as he will
be awakened to, and then let him die,—as die he is
doing and die he must,—under his changed life.

This is the best and all we can do. His game
flies before the white man; we cannot restore it to
him if we would; we would not if we could; it is
his destiny to die; we cannot continue to him his
original, pure barbaric life; he cannot mount to
that of civilization; the mongrel marriage of the
two that he embraces and must submit to, is killing him,—and all we can do is to smooth and make
decent the pathway to his grave. All this is possible; and it need not cost so much as the mixed

state of war and bargaining that we have heretofore pursued. In the beginning there must be the display and the use of power to unlearn in the Indians the false ideas our alternately cowardly bargaining and cowardly bullying policy towards them has engendered; but once inaugurated, it will be simple and successful,—it will give us both peace and protection, and the Indians an easier path to the grave than lies before them now. More briefly and soldierly, General Sherman, now alive at last to the true nature of the question, expresses the new and necessary policy: "Peace and protection to the Indians upon the reservations; war and extermination if found off from them."

But to get back to our camp and ourselves. The scare wore off under the tonic of a cool, clear morning, with splendid visions of fresh fields of snow glancing in the sunlight, the arrival of our load of rifles and Indian goods safe, a good breakfast of trout and Governor Hunt's best griddle-cakes, and the following summons to horse for the Twin Lakes. Never party moved out of camp more gladly; and a few miles farther on, the Arkansas valley welcomed us into a new country, full of the light and the freshness and the joy of a newly awakened nature. There was a California roll to the hills that led down to the river; the sage bush that covered them was greener and more stalwart than that of the Middle Park; and the river bottom held a deeper toned grass, and was alive with grazing cattle; while the Sahwatch range of mountains, that divides the Arkansas valley from the Pacific waters, was continu-

ously higher than any we had yet looked up to, and
its bold majestic peaks bore and brought far down
their middles that thin new snow, which is such a
touching type of purity, and is never seen without
a real enthusiasm. Governor Bross and Vice-President Colfax, who had been off spending the night
among the miners of an upper gulch, greeted us,
too, with felicitations on our safety, and with a company of volunteer cavalry, that did not desert us
until all apprehensions of danger had passed away.

Crossing the river, descending the valley, and
then turning up among the western hills, over one,
two lines of them, racing and roystering along with
our new companions, and in our new joys, we suddenly came out over the Twin Lakes, and stopped.
The scene was, indeed, enchanting. At our feet, a
half a mile away, was the lower of two as fine sheets
of water as mountain ever shadowed, or wind rip-
pled, or sun illuminated. They took their places
at once in the goodly company of the Cumberland
Lakes of England, of Lucerne in Switzerland, of
Como and Laggiore in north Italy, of Tahoe and
Donner in California, and no second rank among
them all. One is about three miles by a mile and
a half; the other say two miles by one; and only a
fifty-rod belt of grass and grove separates them.
Above them on two sides sharply rise,—dark with
trees and rocks until the snow caps with white,—
the mountains of the range; sparsely-wooded hills
of grass and sage bush mount gracefully in succes-
sive benches on a third,—it was over these that we
came into their presence; while to the south a nar-

row, broken valley, pushed rapidly by the mountains towards the Arkansas, carries their outlet stream to its home in the main river. Clear, hard, sandy beaches alternate with walls of rock and low marshy meadows in making the immediate surroundings of both lakes. The waters are purity itself, and trout abound in them.

Here we camped for that and the next day, which was Sunday; restored our Indian-broken nerves; caught trout and picked raspberries; bathed in the lakes; rode up and around them; looked into their waters, and on over them to the mountains,—first green, then blue, then black, finally white, and then higher to clouds, as changing in color under storm, under sun, under moon, under lightning. Every variety of scene, every change and combination of cloud and color were offered us in these two days; and we worshiped, as it were, at the very fountains of beauty, where its every element in nature lay around, before, and above us.

Also, not to live forever in poetry, we patched our clothes, greased our boots, washed our handkerchiefs and towels,—one would dry while another was being washed, in the dry, breezy air,—and ate boiled onions and raspberry short-cake to repletion. Bayard Taylor's letters are at least a guide to the opportunities for good dinners in Colorado; and ostensibly with the purpose to explore the lakes, and see the falls in the river above, possibly with a thought to fall upon such hospitality as he experienced in the little neighboring village of Dalton,—another collection of vacant cabins, with a new

6*

court-house, and only two occupied tenements,— a few of us stole quietly off for a Sunday excursion.

We circled the lakes, as beautiful in detail as in grand effect; picked out many a charming camping-ground for future visits; found along the shores one or two resident families, and a tent with a stove-pipe through it, where a Chicago invalid was spending the summer, gaining vigorous strength and permanent health, and drying quantities of trout,— think of trout so plenty as to suggest drying them! —followed up the bed of the stream two miles or more above the lakes to a very pretty waterfall, and a deep pool, worn out of solid rock, thick with visible trout, whom we could poke with long sticks, but could not seduce with fattest of grasshoppers; lunched off the mountain raspberry vines; tracked a grizzly bear; and looked up the far-stretching gorge through rocks and bushes and vines that were very seducing,—but came back to Dalton in time to get our invitation to dinner. There was white table-cloth, and chairs, and fresh beefsteak, and mealy potatoes, and soft onions, and cream for coffee, and raspberry short-cake "to kill," and a lady and gentleman for hostess and host; everything and more and better even than Taylor had two years before. Going back by the lakes to camp just at sunset, they were in their best estate of color, of light and shade; and water and mountain and sky met and mingled, and led on the eye from one glory to another, till the joy of the spirit overcame and subdued and elevated the satisfaction of the senses.

X.

FROM THE TWIN LAKES TO DENVER.

Down the Arkansas Valley—A Picturesque Scene—A Sensation—
Over into South Park—Who were with us, and How we Made
Camp and Spent the Night—Governor Bross Grinding Coffee—
Governor Hunt's "Slapjacks"—An Evening in Camp with the
Indians—Out of the Park, and into the Plains—Through "the
Garden of the Gods"—Grand Entree into Denver.

DENVER, Colorado, September, 1868.

WE entered the Arkansas valley so far up that
its head was visible. It leads to the lowest pass in
all the mountains over to the Pacific slope, not rising above the timber line. Like all the passes of
the range, it is ambitious of a railroad, and certainly
seems more reasonably so than many others. But
for many years to come our continental railroads
will find lower and smoother paths both north and
south of Colorado.

The plan of our journey was to go from the
Twin Lakes down the Arkansas, around the outside of South Park, so nearly as the rock-bound
banks of the river would allow, through Canon City
and Colorado City, and up by the Plains, under the
eastern line of the mountains, to Denver. Thus we
should have circuited all the great central portions

of the state, and except San Luis Park, which we should have left in the south, have seen all the principal centers of her population, all the distinguishing features of her geography and her natural beauty. But this would have taken us directly into the path of the now rampantly hostile Indians; so we drew in our lines, and made a narrower circle across the South Park, and up to Denver. We lost little or nothing that was distinctive, though some repetitions and modifications of beautiful scenery already or to be made familiar to us. But I urge all who come after us to follow our intended route, and even to extend their trip over into San Luis Park. Here, though the testimony is contradictory, will be found a country rich in beauty and resources, and with some features not characteristic of the other great Parks.

First we rode some twelve miles down the valley. With a mounted escort of about twenty gallant young gold miners, and the addition of two or three camping parties that sought our company home as a sedative to the nervousness of the Indian stories, we made up a grand "outfit." All together, there were from seventy-five to one hundred persons, and as many animals, as it moved back over the mountains into South Park again. The first eight miles were through a broken, hilly country, the mountains coming down to the river on each side in great gashes or rolls, occasionally a broad inclined plain, frequently a dry ravine. The soil was light and cold, and sage bush and coarse grass and thin forests were its products, other than gold. Of the latter it holds in deposit a plentiful sprinkling almost everywhere; and we passed the prosperous mining villages of Granite and Cash Creek, their peoples tearing up the ground all about in eager search for the precious metal.

Little canyons and big canyons drove our road away from the river and over hills and bluffs for much of these eight miles; but at the end we came down into a wider and richer opening, and there spread before us a fine agricultural section, the garden of the upper Arkansas. For thirty-five miles now, the river, hugging the hills on the east, lays open a broad, clean, rising plain of from one to ten miles in width, before the rocks and forests of the western mountains begin. Beyond these thirty-five miles, the river canyons again for a long course, and farming is at an end, and travel down the valley is turned off into South Park till the stream emerges again from its rock embrasures. Tributaries of the main stream slash and fertilize this great meadow; and it bears large crops of grain, grass and roots. Some twenty farmers have brought under profitable cultivation about seven hundred acres of this valley; the mines in the valleys above and over in South Park furnish the markets; a Frenchman, one of the first of these ranchmen, and whose bread and milk we devoured as we went by, returned an income of from twelve to fifteen thousand dollars two years ago, as the results of a single season's farming, crops being good and prices high; and, spite of grasshoppers and drouth, the business is uniformly more successful than mining.

Crossing the river through the hospitable Frenchman's grounds, we turned up the hills, and began to
leave this inviting country almost as soon as we
had entered it.   It beckoned us back by scenes of
exquisite beauty, clothed in warm sunshine, and at
every convenient spot in the ascending hills, we
lingered for longing looks, up and, down, and ·
across its lines.   All around on the lower hills,
down to the river, guarding its passage, were
magnificent ruins of mountains; huge boulders;
fantastic shaped columns; lines of palisades; the
kernels which water could not wash nor abrasion
wear away; groves of rocks; fortresses upon the
river shore,—the Rhine is not more thickly peopled
with ruined castles; with pines and aspens and
coarse bushes growing upon and among them all,
including a new species, called *pinyon*, a stunted,
sprawling, thick-growing pine, looking, as set in a
grove a little way off, like an old apple orchard.
Starting from the opposite bank, the open, rising
meadow, a great inclined plain of gray and green,
stretching miles away up the sides of the grand
Sahwatch Mountains, whose tops formed a line of
snow fields that overlooked and cooled the whole
warm scene of sunshine and life below.   Up and
down hills we toiled all the afternoon, refreshed only
and yet tantalized by occasional glimpses of the
beautiful valley behind, which seemed to spread
out all its beauty of form, of scene, of color, to har-
row us for so early deserting it.

The only other sensation of the afternoon's ride
was the sudden dashing into our line from behind

of a dozen or twenty Ute chiefs and warriors. As we had not learned to know one kind of Indians from another, their galloping in among us stirred the blood a trifle; but we soon found they were friends, and pairing off among our mounted men, they were grunting and gesticulating their story into all our ears. They proved to be the leaders of a band of Utes living down in the San Luis Park country, who had learned, in the mysterious and speedy manner of savages and wildernesses, of the uprising of the hostile Indians of the Plains, and of the presence of Governor Hunt and our party in this region, and so, traveling day and night, they had hurried up to meet us, and see if they were wanted, either to protect us, or take the field against their and our enemies. Not without a selfish thought, too, perhaps, for blankets and beef. They camped with us that night, were well-fed and well-promised, and went back home the next day. The Governor had neither authority nor means to put them into the field against the Plain Indians; nor was it clear that there was any occasion for it. ·

We pushed up near to the tops of the mountains, riding far into the evening, before camping, and finally pitched our tents in a great meadow, heavy with grass, and interspersed with little wooded knolls, within and around one of which we built our fires and laid our blankets for the night. We needed them all, for it was dreary cold before morning, and water froze in our cups on the way from the brook half a mile off. But the forenoon's sun and saddle brought summer warmth back; and

we were not long in getting óver the range and
down into South Park. We entered it about at the
middle, and it seemed tamer and less green than
in the upper sections. Alkali and salt deposits
whitened the surface in great patches, and so rich
are the springs with salt at one spot, that a large
establishment for evaporating the water and making salt is in operation, and holds a profitable mo-
nopoly of the salt market of the state. We made
a fine noon camp by one of the everlasting Plattes,
and trout-catching was brisk for an hour.

Here, too, we had another Indian raid,—the out-
posts of our old Middle Park Utes, who had heard
the story of the Plain Indians coming up into the
South Park, and moved over in a body to dispos-
sess them, came wildly and joyfully riding in upon
us, a dozen or two, with some white friends from
Fairplay. So our escort doubled, and we trav-
eled across the Park with as large and as motley
a retinue as ever Oriental prince moved among
over the deserts of Asia. Only, with true American individuality, we scattered wildly about, and
lingered or hurried at pleasure over the wide open
plains, dotted with occasional hill and lake, the latter repeated by mirage in the distance, or by the
deceptive resemblance of an alkali field, and circled
by the far-distant, far-reaching mountains. Everything else failing or fatiguing, from sheer abundance,—mountain, field, grass, forest, color, the atmosphere remained, a feeling of beauty that minis-
tered to several senses without ever palling the
appetite of either.

We made grand camp that night about a mile beyond Fairplay, on a gently sloping plateau, backed
by a thick aspen grove, watered at its base by a
fresh stream, fronted by the broad Park meadows,
looking towards sundown, and taking the best light
of the full moon through its nightly circle of the
horizon. The dozen or twenty Utes enlisted to go
through with us to Denver, and made a camp for
themselves a few rods away among the trees. The
mounted men were usually the first in camp; they
stripped their animals of saddles and bridles and
blankets, and sent them galloping off for grass and
water. As fast as the wagons came up, they took
their places in the grand circle of the camp-ground,
and were unloaded of tents, baggage and provisions, and their horses loosened to join the others.
Smooth spots were chosen for the tents in a semicircle, and the tents put up by the most adroit in
that business. There was one for Governor Hunt
and his family; another for Mr. Witter and his,
consisting of himself, his wife (Mr. Colfax's sister),
a babe eight weeks old,—think of that, you tender
mothers in four-walled and ·close-roofed houses in
civilization!—and Mr. Colfax's mother and father;
a third for the young ladies; Governor Bross and
the Vice-President used one of the large covered
wagons for lodgings; my friend Lord and myself
had a little tent by ourselves; and the rest, des-
pising such paltry interventions of effeminacy, lay
around in the softest, shadiest places, under the
wagons, under trees, always near the fires. The
little sheet-iron cooking-stoves, one for each of the

two messes into which our original party was divided, were simultaneously planted and fired up. The open fires were located, and the Vice-President, Governor Bross, Mr. Thomas of the Rocky Mountain News, and any other idle and otherwise incompetent persons were detailed to fetch wood for them.   Soon a huge fire blazed in front of each tent.   Then the wood-haulers became water-carriers.   Next the fastidious made their toilets; and Governor Hunt called for assistant cooks.

This night we were to have an extra meal.   To start with, and especially to provide quantity for the capacious Indian stomachs, a herd of cattle were driven up from the meadow, and Mr. Curtis, the Indian interpreter, passing them in review, rifle in hand, and, choosing a fat young cow, sent a ball unerringly into her forehead, and she fell dead instantly.   It was the first time I had ever seen this speedy, humane manner of butchering; and Mr. Bergh, the anti-cruelty man, ought to demand its universal use.   The animal was soon cut up, and a few choice pieces brought to our camp, but the Indians carried off the bulk to theirs, and, with forked sticks and open fire, and a little salt, were soon filling up their waste places.   The village furnished us cream and fresh supplies of sugar.   Soon we had beefsteak frying, mush and milk in proper progress, oyster soup and tomatoes stewing, hominy warming, a huge section of ribs of beef roasting on a forked stick before the fire, coffee and tea brewing, biscuits baking at one mess, and slapjacks browning at another.   Governor Bross earned his supper by grinding coffee for half an hour, and after-wards, his hand having grown supple, you could have seen him, seated on an empty whisky-keg, turning the griddle-cakes to perfection; and your correspondent won his glory and victual by mak-ing the "long-sweetening," *i. e.* white sugar melted into a permanent syrup. Then there were canned peaches and raspberries for dessert. All this, seated on our haunches on the ground or on bended knees around the board and box that served for tables, each with a tin plate and cup, and knife and fork and spoon to match, and all with appetites worthy the food. We generally "boarded around," that is ate at the mess which happened to have the most inviting meal, and as there is no knowledge so satisfactory as the experimental on such a subject, it commonly resulted in our eating at both. It is surprising how excellent food can be had in such a camping expedition with a little painstaking and tact in providing and cooking. Governor Hunt was master of all the arts of camp-life, and under his care we "fared sumptuously every day." The slap-jacks and their "long-sweetening" were an incom-parable dish, and took the place of bread at Gov-ernor Hunt's table.

Supper over, and the dishes washed, in which last operation "equal rights" were sometimes allowed the women, all gathered around the central camp-fires, with shawls, buffalo robes and blankets for protection from the ground; our friends traveling in company, who had made separate camps adjoin-ing, came over to spend the evening; to-night our

escort party from the Arkansas valley had supped
with us, and were about to say farewell; and their
Indian successors, having become happy and hilarious, were invited and welcomed into the circle; and
thus re-enforced and diversified, we made a gala
night of it.   It was a very curious scene indeed.
The blaze of the camp-fire contrasted sharply with
the light of the moon, and brought out in fine relief all the hundred varying faces and strange costumes gathered around.   Speeches were made and
songs sung; Mr. Colfax addressed the Utes, and
his words were interpreted to them by Mr. Curtis,
and the reply of their chief to us; and then we
called for songs from them.   Stimulated by a pile
of white sugar that Governor Hunt threw down at
their feet, they got up and responded with spirit.
Standing in a row, shoulders touching, and sway-
ing to and fro in a long line by one motion, they
chanted in a low, guttural way, all on one key, and
only musical as it was correct monotone.   Then
there were more songs and sentiments from the
whites; the Indians were dismissed; our kind friends
from the Arkansas said good-by; and soon the fires
of camp were dull, and all its life still in sleep,—a
sleep of trust and safety, there under the open sky,
with a village of all sorts of people a mile away,
and a band of savages within six rods.   It was all
so incongruous and anomalous to our home thought
and life; and yet we felt as safe, and were as
safe, as in double-bolted houses on police-patrolled
streets.   Only the contrasts forced themselves into
the wakeful moments of night and morning, as we

turned over and refastened the blankets, and piled
more baggage over chilly feet, and peered out into
the dead stillness of the camp, broken may-be by
the dull snoring of a heavy sleeper, and the far-off
browsing of a greedy mule; sounds brought near
and made loud by the hush of human life, and the
reign of nature's peace.

Out of the Park and into the hills that separate
it from the Plains the next day. The way was
familiar, the road for the most part good. We scattered along, two or three together, through five or
six miles; closing up for lunch, and again for night
camp. Our Indian escort, familiar with every rod
of the country, roamed at will, taking short cuts over
the hills, and appearing first in the rear, then far in
advance. We had a beautiful camp, after twenty-
five miles ride, in a narrow but long little valley,
that bowed the sun out at one end, as it welcomed
the moon up at the other. The next day, too, all
among the hills, riding another twenty-five miles;
the roads improving; ranches thickening,—no lack
now of buttermilk or cream; travelers grew numerous; daily newspapers coming in; and the end
dawning. It was a pleasant mountain country, open,
free, lightly wooded, abundantly watered, and the valleys rich for grass and grain. The streams, too, hold
trout, and the hills are thick with raspberries,—it is
up here that the Denverites come for their briefer
mountain excursions, and this is the common road
for commerce and for pleasure into the South Park.

Our night camp now was the last of the excursion. It was near the junction of the roads lead-

ing to Denver by the Plains and to Idaho through the mountains.   There was a rivalry among the cooking-stoves for the best farewell supper; but the slapjacks gave Governor Hunt the victory,— there was no equalling, no resisting them.   Around the camp-fire, we "talked it over;" hilarious with a vein of sadness ; humorous with a touch of pathos ; Mr. Colfax made his excellent speech, beginning, "this is the saddest moment of my life;" we sang auld-lang-syne, and prepared for an early start in the morning.

The breakfast dishes were packed dirty,—"after us the Deluge,"—and camp was broken by eight o'clock with the cry, " Ho, for Denver."   The going out of the mountains was very fine.   The several miles through Turkey Creek Canyon, the road winding along with the stream at the bottom of a high gorge of rocks, were fresh and exhilarating ; we had gone around canyons before, painfully and laboriously ; now to follow one by a narrow but firm road offered new and picturesque views.   This was not unlike the Via Mala of Switzerland ; and coming out, the road circled a high precipitous hill midway in its side, an expensive and excellent bit of road-making, such as is rarely seen anywhere in America.

Here we overlooked the grand ocean of the Plains, and came upon the struggles of nature to leave off mountain and begin plain.   Along here, as at other points below, there seems to have been an especial and antagonistic fold thrown up almost abruptly from the level plain.   Pike's Peak, which is distinct from the main range, is the chief endeavor or culmination of this throe of the formation. And around it, as here, are grouped monuments or remains of mountains, alike grotesque, commanding, impressive; taking all shapes, and giving the thought that somebody greater and higher than man had made here familiar home. The collection of these ruins near Pike's Peak and Colorado City, which we missed seeing because of the Indian war, is called "The Garden of the Gods," and the name not unfitly clothes the impression they make. They are not boulders or piles of rock, but what is left of mountains washed and worn away by waters and winds. The body is a fine reddish granite; and they stand sentinelled about upon the bare closing bluffs of the hills, with forms of such majesty and such personality, as arouses one's wonder and deepens curiosity into awe.

Down into the last ravine, and out upon the long' rolls of the Plains. The Platte and its branches wind with their gardens of grain and their groves of trees about in the far distance, making a pleasantly variegated map of green of the vast picture. Bear Creek especially offers a charming principality of its own. And far in the thin haze the steeples and blocks of Denver stand upon the sky. Herds of grazing cattle are scattered along on both sides of the road; and with a common hunger for home and civilization, beasts and drivers spur each other into rapid gait. Our day's ride of twenty-five miles is finished by two o'clock, and we stop before entering the town to "serry the ranks," and try the unaccustomed draughts of a suburban brewery.

A circus would have been a poor show compared to the procession that then passed into Denver. First were the faithful Utes, gay with bright blankets and yellow and red paint; a bride among them, beaded and bespangled from head to foot; then our own cavaliers and cavalieresses, their plumage not over gay after a fortnight's mountain use, their animals worn and sorry from hard riding and no oats; next.carriages, ambulances and baggage-wagons, out of which peered flapping sun bonnets and browned faces, with every other wheel bound in huge sticks from the forest to keep them from dropping to pieces; and finally Governor Evans's carriage, altogether minus two wheels, and just lifted from the ground by two poles that dragged their slow length along behind. Despite the solemnity of the town over the Indian raids; despite the dignity of demeanor due to high officials, Ute chiefs, Colorado chiefs, Illinois chiefs, Washington fathers,—the street broke into a horse, neigh a mule laugh that rolled along from block to block, and turned the back doors out in affright lest Cherry Creek had come to town again. And then we were dismissed to assure our friends of our identity, and reconstruct ourselves.

XI.

MINES, MINING AND MINERS.

Review of the Mining Interests of Colorado—Present Condition of Affairs in the Quartz Centers—Central City, Georgetown, Mill City, Empire City, etc.—Renewal of Gulch-Mining, its Profits, and its Promises—Present Yield of Gold and Silver, and its Certain Increase—Population of Colorado, and the Idiosyncracies of its Miners.

DENVER, Colorado, September, 1868.

IT remains for me to speak of the industrial interests, growth, prosperity, and promise, of Colorado. These have only been incidentally alluded to so far; but they deserve special exhibition. The change in its material affairs and prospects, since we were here three years ago, is most marked and healthy. Then, the original era of speculation, of waste, of careless and unintelligent work, and as little of it as possible, of living by wit instead of labor, of reliance upon eastern capital instead of home industry, was, if not at its hight, still reigning, but with signs of decay and threatening despair. The next two years, 1866 and 1867, affairs became desperate; the population shrunk; mines were abandoned; mills stopped; eastern capital, tired of waiting for promised returns, dried

7

up its fountains; and the secrets of the rich ores seemed unfathomable. Residents, who could not get away, were put to their trumps for a living; and economy and work were enforced upon all. Thus weeded out, thus stimulated, the population fell back on the certainties; such mining as was obviously remunerative was continued; the doubtful and losing abandoned; the old and simple dirt washing for gold was resumed, and followed with more care; and farming rose in respectability and promise. The discovery and opening of specially rich silver mines near Georgetown kept hope and courage alive, and freshened speculation in a new quarter; but the main fact of the new era was that the people went to work, became self-reliant, and, believing that they "had a good thing" out here, undertook to prove it to the world by intelligent and economic industry.

These were the kernel years of Colorado; they proved her; they have made her. Her gold product went down, probably, to a million dollars say, in each of 1866 and 1867; but it began at once, under the new order of things, to rise; and agriculture also at once shot up and ahead, and directly assumed, as it has in California, the place of the first interest, the great wealth. No more flour, no more corn, no more potatoes at six cents to twelve cents a pound freight, from the Missouri River; in one year Colorado became self-supporting in food; in the second an exporter, the feeder of Montana, the contractor for the government posts and the Pacific Railroad; and now, in the third year,

with food cheaper than in "the States," she forces
the Mississippi and Missouri valleys to keep their
produce at home or send it East. She feeds the
whole line of the Pacific Railroad this side the continental divide, and has even been sending some of
her vegetables to Omaha. Her gold and silver
product is up to at least two millions this year, got
out at a profit of from twenty-five to fifty per cent.,
is now at the rate of nearly if not quite three millions, and will certainly surpass that sum in 1869.
Her agricultural products must be twice as much
at least, certainly four millions for 1868, and perhaps six millions; though it is difficult to make
as certain estimates in this particular, and the Indians have worked great mischief with the ingather-
ing of the crops this fall.

Central City, in the midst of the mountains on
the north branch of Clear Creek, continues to be
the center of the gold quartz-mining; and business
there was never more healthily prosperous than
now. All its stamp mills are in operation, and more
are being erected; for after wearily waiting through
two or three years for more effective processes for
reducing the ores, their owners have set these in
operation again, simplified, perfected and econo-
mized their working, and, from about one hundred
and forty mills and seven hundred and fifty stamps,
are now producing near fifty thousand dollars of
gold a week, at a cost for both mining and milling
of from two-thirds to three-quarters that sum. Another season will see say fifty mills and one thousand stamps at work in this valley. The most

valuable ores of the neighboring mines are not put through this process, but are sold at about one hundred dollars a ton to Professor Hill's smelting or Swansea works, now established here, and working the richer and sulphuretted ores with an economy and completeness that the plain stamp mills cannot do. The ores worked in the latter form the principal product of the mines, and produce under the stamps about twenty-five dollars a ton, while the cost for mining and milling is about fifteen dollars. If steam is used the cost goes up to twenty dollars. The Swansea and the plain stamp mill are the only "processes" now in use in this valley. Professor Hill has proved the success and profit of the former, at least for all high-class ores. He is giving from eighty to one hundred and twenty-five dollars a ton for such ore, and probably makes from thirty to forty dollars a ton on it; and his purchases amount to some twenty thousand dollars a month. He is already doubling his furnaces. But the problem is to apply his process profitably to lower class ores; to such as hold from twenty-five to fifty dollars a ton, and of which there are almost literally mountains in Colorado. The free or simple gold ores of this grade can be worked well enough by stamps and amalgamation, as in Central City and California, and the cost thereof can be ultimately reduced to probably one-half of present prices; but these constitute only a fraction of the rich ores of Colorado. Most of them hold both silver and gold, combined with sulphurets of iron, and a process which gets one leaves the other, except, of course, smelting, which at present is too expensive for any but highly-freighted ores. This is why thousands of mines are unworked to-day; why scores of mills with unperfected processes, or plain stamps, stand idle, rotting and rusting in all parts of the territory; and why deserted cabins and vacant villages lie scattered in all the valleys about,—telling their tragic tales of loss and disappointment, monuments of the enthusiasm and the credulity of miner and capitalist, who labored and invested wildly and before their time.

Some silver mine discoveries have recently been made in the Central City region; indeed, there is silver in all the gold ores, and gold in all the silver ores of the territory, and lead and copper in most besides; but the head-quarters of the silver business is at Georgetown, ten or a dozen miles over the mountains from Central City, at the head of the south branch of Clear Creek. Around and above this now thriving and most beautifully located of the principal mining villages of Colorado; at nine thousand, ten thousand, on even to twelve and thirteen thousand feet above the sea level, almost unapproachable save in summer, and then only by pack mules or on foot, are many marvelously rich silver veins in the rocks. Hundreds of mines have been opened; but only a dozen or twenty are now being actually worked with profitable results. The rest await purchasers from their "prospectors," or capital to develop them. The ore from the leading mines ranges from one hundred to one thousand dollars a ton. Only two mills for reducing the ore are in operation; one treats the second class ore, such as will average say two hundred dollars a ton, reducing it by crushing or stamping, then washing with salt to oxydize it, and then amalgamating with quicksilver, at a cost of from fifty to one hundred dollars a ton; and the other smelting the higher priced ores, at a cost probably of one hundred to two hundred dollars a ton. The latter establishment buys outright most of the ore it reduces, and has paid all the way from five hundred to six hundred and seventy-five dollars a ton for it. Both processes get out from seventy-five to ninety per cent of the assay value of the ore; but they are imperfect and expensive, and much of the best ore is sent East for treatment. The Equator mine, owned by a party of railroad men from Chicago, is one of the two or three prizes here, and sends its first-class ore, worth from nine hundred to one thousand dollars a ton, all the way to Newark, N. J., to be reduced. Thirty tons were packed for shipment the day I was there. The superior yield under the closer and more economical treatment at Newark more than pays for the freight, which is but forty-eight dollars a ton. The Equator mine claims to have yielded one hundred thousand dollars' worth of ore this season, and brags of a million next. Only a portion of its ore taken out is yet worked. There are several, perhaps half a dozen other mines nearly as good as this.

Georgetown now has a population of about three thousand, and the best hotel in the territory. It is one of the places that every tourist should visit, partly for its silver mines, partly because the road to it up the South Clear Creek is through one of the most interesting sections of the mountains, and partly that it is the starting-point for the ascension of Gray's Peaks. The traveler can go up to the top of that mountain and back to Georgetown between breakfast and supper; and if he will not take his tour by the Snake and Blue Rivers to the Middle or South Park, he should certainly make this day's excursion from Georgetown. Central City and its neighborhood are much less interesting to the mere pleasure traveler. That town, with its four thousand or five thousand inhabitants, is crowded into a narrow gulch, rather than valley, torn with floods, and dirty with the debris of mills and mines that spread themselves over everything.

Scattered about, in Boulder District, on the Snake, over on the Upper Arkansas, up among the gulches of the South Park hills, are a few more quartz mills, some in operation, more not; but the principal business of quartz mining is done in the sections I have named, in Gilpin and Clear Creek counties. Mill City, Empire, and Idaho are villages in this section, with their mines and mills, doing a little something, struggling to prove their capacity, but hardly in a single case making money, partly because of the poverty of the ore, but chiefly because it is refractory, and will not yield up its possessions to any known and reasonably cheap process. Time, patience, and cheaper labor will bring good results out of many of these investments; but others will have to go to swell the great number of failures that stand confessed all over this as all over every other mining country.

There are great tunneling schemes proposed or started in the Georgetown silver district, by which the various ore veins of a single mountain are to be cut deep down in their depths, and their wealth brought out of a single mouth in the valley, at a much cheaper rate than by digging down from the top on the vein's course and hauling up. The "Burleigh drill" from Massachusetts, that has been in use in the Hoosac tunnel, has been introduced here for this purpose; and successful mining on a grand scale will soon take this form, not only here, but in Nevada, and indeed in most of our mining States.

The other form of mining, known as gulch-mining or dirt-washing, is increasing again, and has employed full three hundred men this season. Fifty to seventy-five of these are at work in the Clear Creek and Boulder valleys; but the great body of them are scattered through Park, Lake, and Summit counties, on the Snake and other tributaries of the Blue River; on the upper Plattes in South Park; and on the upper Arkansas and its side valleys. They have averaged twelve dollars a day to a man; but the season for this kind of mining is less than half the year, in some places because of ice and snow; in most for lack of water. The year's product from gulch-mining will certainly foot up half a million dollars, probably a hundred thousand more. New gulches and fresh "bars," or deposits of sand, brought down from the hills by the streams, have been opened this year in preparation for another year's work; and it is not unreasonable to look for a million dollars from gulch-mining next year.

These figures seem small compared with the amounts reported to be got out in the years following the first gold discoveries in 1859,—in '60 to '64,—when one year's production ran up as high as six or eight millions, and for several years averaged probably four; when hundreds if not thousands of eager miners were gathered in a single gulch, and ran over its sands with a reckless waste, taking off the cream of the deposits, and then moving on to new places, and, finally exhausting both their own first enthusiasm, and all the best or most obvious chances, turning away in disgust at a "played out" territory. But the business is now resumed in a more systematic, intelligent and economical way; labor is cheaper; miners are satisfied with more moderate returns; and there is really almost no limit to these valleys and banks, under the hills and along the rivers, whose sands and gravel hold specks of gold in sufficient quantity to pay for washing over. An intelligent investigator of the subject tells me that the whole of South Park would pay three to four dollars a day for the labor of washing it over. But I pray it may not be done while I live to come to these Mountains and the Parks; for gold-washing leaves a terrible waste in its track.

In the valley of the Blue and its tributaries, more extensive works for gulch-mining exist than in any other district; there, not less than eighty-four miles

of ditches to bring water to wash out the gold with
have been constructed, and the amount of water
they carry in the aggregate is eight thousand seven
hundred and fifty inches.   One of these ditches is
eleven miles long; two others seven miles each;
another five, and so on; and they cost from one
thousand to .twelve hundred dollars a mile.   Says
Mr. Thomas of the Rocky Mountain News, from
whose careful and elaborate investigations this
summer and fall, I draw many of the facts of this
letter:—"The facilities and opportunities for gulch-
mining in this county (Summit) are equal if not superior to any in Colorado.   Many of the gulches,
now worked, will last for years to come, while much
ground remains yet untouched.   The Blue River
will pay for ten miles or more, at the rate of five to
ten dollars per day to the man.   Many places will
pay from three to five dollars per day to the man,
and will be worked when labor becomes lower and
living cheaper."

In the Granite district of the Upper Arkansas,
quartz gold is found in simple combinations, or
"free," as in California, which can be mined and
reduced for eight to ten dollars a ton, while it yields
from fifteen to one hundred dollars; but these are
ores from near the surface, and it is yet a problem
whether they will not change on getting down in
the veins, as in other Colorado mines, and become
"refractory," and impossible of working at a profit
by any yet known process.

The Cinnamon mines, just over the southern border in New Mexico, have attracted much attention

for the last two years. Several quartz mills are in operation there, but the main yield, so far, is from the gulches, and the total product this year is about a quarter of a million dollars. San Luis Park, too, is believed to be rich in mineral deposits; some promising discoveries have already been made there; and indeed in almost every quarter of the state are the beginnings of developments that inspire great faiths, each in its own particular circle of prospectors and prophets.

There is apparently no limit, in fact, to the growth of the mineral interests of Colorado. The product this year is from two millions to two and a half; next year it will be at least a million more, perhaps a million and a half, or four millions; and the increase will go on indefinitely. For the business is now taken hold of in the right way; pursued for the most part on strictly business principles; and every year must show improvements in the ways and means of mining and treating the ores. The mountains are just full of ores holding fifteen to fifty dollars' worth of the metals per ton; and the only question, as to the amount to be got out, is one of labor and cost as compared with the profits of other pursuits.

The settled population of Colorado is now at least fifty thousand, perhaps sixty thousand. About one-quarter is Mexican, all in the southern section, and ignorant and debased to a shameful degree. The rest are as good a population as any new state can boast of. They are drawn from all eastern sources; but the New England leaven, though possibly not the New England personality, is domi-

nant in their ambition, their education, their morality, their progressive spirituality. The pioneer
miners, the "prospectors," are a class of characters
by themselves. Properly they never mine ; to dig·
out and reduce ore is not their vocation ; but they
discover and open mines, and sell them, if they
can ; at any rate move on to discover others. Men
of intelligence, often cultivated, generally handsome, mostly moral, high-toned and gallant by
nature, sustained by a faith that seems imperish-
able, putting their last dollar, their only horse, possibly their best blanket, into a hole that invites
their hopes, working for wages only to get more
means to live while they prospect anew and further, they suffer much, and yet enjoy a great deal.
Faith is comfort, and that is theirs ; they will
"strike it rich" some day ; and then, and not till
then, will they go back to the old Ohio, Pennsylvania or New England homes, and cheer the fading eyes of fathers and mothers, and claim the
patient-waiting, sad-hearted girls, to whom they
pledged their youthful loves. The vicious and
the loafers, the gamblers and the murderers, have
mostly "moved on ;" what is left is chiefly golden
material ; and the men and the mines and farms of
Colorado, all alike and together, are in a healthy
and promising condition, and insure for her a large
growth and a generous future. The two things
she lacketh chiefly now are appreciation at the
East and women ; what she has of both are excellent, but in short supply ; but the Railroad will
speedily fill the vacuums.

XII.

THE AGRICULTURE OF COLORADO.

The Farming Interests of Colorado; their Great Attainment and
Greater Promise—Details of the Harvest and of Prices—Stock-
Raising—The Birth and Growth of Manufactures—The Colo-
rado Bread—Coal and Iron—Professor Agassiz among the
Mountains, looking after his Glaciers—End of the Vacation
—Summing Up of its Experiences—Colorado the Switzerland
of America—How to Travel There.

DENVER, Colorado, September, 1868.

INEXHAUSTIBLE as is Colorado's mineral wealth;
progressive as henceforth its development; pre-
dominant and extensive as are its mountains; high
even as are its valleys and plains,—in spite of all
seeming impossibilities and rivalries, Agriculture is
already and is destined always to be its dominant
interest. Hence my faith in its prosperity and its
influence among the central states of the Continent. For agriculture is the basis of wealth, of
power, of morality; it is the conservative element
of all national and political and social growth; it
steadies, preserves, purifies, elevates. Full one-
third of the territorial extent of Colorado,—though
this third average as high as Mount Washington,
—is fit, more, rich for agricultural purposes. The

grains, the vegetables and the fruits of the temperate zone grow and ripen in profusion; and through the most of it, cattle and sheep can live and fatten the year around without housing or feeding. The immediate valleys or bottom lands of the Arkansas and Platte and Rio Grande and their numerous tributaries, after they debouch from the mountains, are of rich vegetable loams, and need no irrigation. The uplands or plains are of a coarse, sandy loam, rich in the phosphates washed from the minerals of the mountains, and are not much in use yet except for pastures. When cultivated, more or less irrigation is introduced, and probably will always be indispensable for sure crops of roots and vegetables; but for the small, hard grains, I have no idea it will be generally found necessary. It is a comparatively dry climate, indeed; but showers are frequent, and extend over a considerable part of the spring and summer.

At a rough estimate, the agricultural wealth of Colorado last year was a million bushels of corn, half a million of wheat, half a million of barley, oats and vegetables, 50,000 head of cattle, and 75,000 to 100,000 sheep. The increase this year is at least 50 per cent; in the northern counties at least 100. Indeed, the agriculture of the northern counties, between the Pacific Railroad at Cheyenne and Denver, which has grown to be full half that of the whole state, is the development almost entirely of the last three years. South, in the Arkansas and Rio Grande valleys, the farming and the population are older, going back to before the gold discoveries. This is the Spanish-Mexican section, and was formerly a part of New Mexico. Its agriculture is on a large but rough scale, and only the immense crops and the simple habits of the people, chiefly ignorant, degraded Mexicans, permit it to be profitable. The soil yields wonderfully, north and south. There is authentic evidence of 316 bushels of corn to the acre in the neighborhood of Denver this season; 60 to 75 bushels of wheat to the acre are very frequently reported; also 250 bushels of potatoes; and 60 to 70 of both oats and barley. These are exceptional yields, of course, and yet not of single acres, but of whole fields, and on several farms in different counties. Probably 30 bushels is the average product of wheat; of corn·no more, for the hot nights that corn loves are never felt here; of oats say 50, and of barley 40, for the whole state. Exhaustion of the virgin freshness of the soil will tend to decrease these averages in the future; but against that we may safely put improved cultivation and greater care in harvesting.

The melons and vegetables are superb; quality, quantity and size are alike unsurpassed by any garden cultivators in the East. The irrigated gardens of the upper parts of Denver fairly riot in growth of fat vegetables; while the bottom lands of the neighboring valleys are at least equally productive without irrigation. Think of cabbages weighing from 50 to 60 pounds each! And potatoes from 5 to 6 pounds, onions 1 to 2 pounds, and beets 6 to 10! Yet here they grow, and as excellent as big

Let me borrow, in further illustration of the farming development of this country, some statistics
of this year's cultivation in a few of the leading
river valleys north and south.   They are from Mr.
Thomas's personal collections for the Denver News:
The Cache-a-la-Poudre is the most northern side
valley of Colorado, and markets at Cheyenne; it
has at least 200,000 acres of tillable lands, and
probably not 5,000 are in use yet; but among its
chief products this year are 25,000 bushels of oats,
5,000 wheat, 5,000 potatoes, 2,500 corn, 2,500 tons
of hay, and 15,000 to 20,000 pounds of butter.   The
oat crop averaged 48 1-2 bushels per acre; and the
cows have generally paid for themselves in butter
this season.   The Big Thompson, another of the
northern valleys, has about 2,000 acres under cultivation, and yields this year 33,000 bushels potatoes, with an average of 165 bushels per acre cultivated ; 27,000 bushels oats, 8,000 bushels wheat,
3,300 bushels corn, 1,400 tons hay, and 7,500 pounds
of cheese from a single dairy.   One farmer has 700
to 800 head of cattle, and 100 to 200 horses and
colts.   In the Platte valley, for sixty miles north
of Denver, or to the mouth of Cache-a-la-Poudre,
there were raised this year 15,000 bushels wheat,
27,000 bushels oats, 5,000 bushels barley, 3,000
bushels corn, 7,000 bushels potatoes, and 1,500 tons
of hay, and about 23,000 pounds of butter made.   In
the valley of the Platte, south of Denver, twenty
miles long, there are 3,000 acres under cultivation,
nearly half in wheat, and a quarter in oats, with
crops of barley at 66 bushels to the acre, of wheat

70, and of oats 65, and the average being 30 to 35 of wheat, 35 to 40 of oats and barley. Bear Creek, just south of Denver, has 1,225 acres cultivated, divided about as those of the Platte are. In the main valley of the Arkansas are nearly 6,000 acres of cultivated land, half corn, and a third wheat; in Fontaine qui Bouille, a branch of the Arkansas, also 6,000, with almost exactly the same division among crops. The St. Charles, another tributary, cultivates 1,500 acres, half corn, a third wheat, the rest oats. In the Huerfana valley, still another tributary of the Arkansas, are 5,000 acres under tillage, with the usual southern division, corn largely dominating, and here are some of the largest farms in the state, ranging up to 1,500 acres in cultivation, and so requiring but few farmers to make up the total. In this valley, the corn crop averages from 30 to 50 bushels the acre, wheat 20 to 40, and oats 40 to 45. These are but specimens of twice as many valleys above and below Denver, in which farming has been begun, but only begun, yet with such profitable results as insure rapid development.

I now quote the prices of agricultural produce this week at Denver; they will be likely to recede as the crops come into market: Barley 3c. a pound, corn 3 1-2 to 4 1-2c., cheese 20 to 22c., corn meal 5c., eggs 50 to 60c. a dozen, flour $7 to 9 a sack of 100 pounds, oats 3c. a pound, potatoes 2 to 3c. a pound, fresh tomatoes 3c. a pound, wheat 3 3-4c. a pound, cabbages 1c. a pound, butter 45c. a pound retail, chickens $5.50 a dozen, good beef 12 to 15c. a pound. At Cheyenne, on the Pacific Railroad, prices are somewhat higher,—like these, for instance, for vegetables: Cabbages 6 to 8c. a pound, onions 6 to 8c. a pound, turnips 2 to 4c. a pound, beets 5 to 7c. a pound, tomatoes 20 to 25c. a pound, squashes 4 to 7c. a pound, cucumbers 40 to 50c. a dozen. Beef is, on the whole, the cheapest grown and the cheapest selling food here. It costs about half the New York and Boston retail prices.

Stock-raising on the Plains is simple and profitable business. The animals can roam at will, and a single man can tend hundreds. The only enemies are the Indians and the diseases that the Texas cattle bring up from the South. But the former are the great evil; the confusion, danger and loss they have created this season sum up a serious blow not only to stock-raising, but to all farming. Even if the evil is suppressed hereafter, this season's raids are a year's loss to the agricultural interests of Colorado. Many farmers have given up in despair from danger and disaster, and retired from the field; others hesitate and refuse to come, who otherwise would be here at once and in force of capital and energy, to enter upon the business.

These great interests of mining and farming shade naturally into others, and already there are the beginnings of various manufacturing developments, as there are the materials and incentives for such undertakings without stint. Some fifteen or twenty flouring-mills are in operation throughout the state. The Colorado wheat makes a rich hearty flour, bearing a creamy golden tinge; and I have eaten no where else in America better bread than is made from it. There is a baker in Georgetown, whose products are as rich and light as the best of German wheat bread. The wheat will rank with the very best that America produces, and is more like the California grain than that of "the States." Coal mines are abundant, and several are being profitably worked along the lower range of the mountains; as, indeed, they have been found and opened at intervals along the line of the Pacific Railroad over the mountains, and are already supplying its engines with a most excellent fuel,—a hard, dry, brown coal, very pure and free-burning; in Boulder valley and Golden City, iron is being manufactured from native ore; at Golden City, there is a successful manufactory of pottery ware and fire brick; also a paper-mill and a tannery, and three flouring-mills; the state already supplies its own salt; soda deposits are abundant everywhere, and will be a great source of wealth; woolen mills are projected and greatly needed, as wool-growing is the simplest of agricultural pursuits here; a valuable tin mine has been lately discovered and its value proved, up in the mountains; and next year the Railroad will be one of Colorado's possessions, and bring harmony and unity and healthy development to all her growth, social, material, and political. Also, by that time she will be a state, and so responsible for her own government, be it good or bad.

As we go out, Professor Agassiz leads a new party of eastern notables from over the Plains and into the Mountains. He is already seething with enthusiasm; all Brazil was nothing, he says, to what he has seen of natural beauty and scientific revelation in crossing the Plains; but the half is not told him. When he comes face to face with the mountains,—the mountains in perfection and the mountains in ruin,—and their phenomena of parks and wealth of verdure, then indeed he may feel he is among the "Gardens of the Gods." The professor finds abundant materials to sustain his wide-spread glacial theories; all these vast elevated plains, from Missouri River to Mountains, from Montana to Mexico,—the very heart of the Continent,—are but in his eye the deposit of great fields of ice, stretching down from these hills and washing down their hights. What must they have been once to have lost so much and remain so Titanesque!—to be still the Mother Mountains of the Continent?

———

Here rests the record of our Summer Vacation in the Rocky Mountains. The stage ride back to Cheyenne,—now hardened to long journeys and open air life,—was a long eighteen hours' pleasure under warm sun and cool stars; and we tumbled into the tender berths of Pullman's palace car, waiting on the railroad track, at three o'clock in the morning, with a keen gratitude to Colorado and all its kind friends for what rare joy of new-experience and rich hospitality they had given us, and as keen a welcome to steam locomotion, beds, and the near home. Two days of the Pacific and the Northwestern Railroads brought us to Chicago, and there we separated, as we gathered, about the hospitable tables of Governor Bross.

Life was fresher to all of us, new to some, for the health and the sentiment of the thin pure air of the Mountains and the Parks. Their skies and their waters repeat the fabled fountain of perpetual youth. It is to them that America will go, as Europe to Switzerland, for rest and recreation, for new and exhilarating scenes, for pure and bracing air, for pleasure and for health. They offer no wonderful valley like the Yo Semite; no continental river breaking through continental mountains like the Columbia; no cataract like Niagara; no forests like those of the Sierra Nevada range, no nor the equals, in diversified form and color and species, of those of New England or of Pennsylvania; and yet I am greatly mistaken if the verdict of more familiar acquaintance by the American people with America is not, that here,—among these central ranges of continental mountains and these great companion parks, within this wedded circle of majestic hill and majestic plain, under these skies of purity, and in this atmosphere of elixir, lies the pleasure-ground and health-home of the nation.

Smoother ways will soon be provided, but no philosophic or accustomed traveler need wait for them. The true aroma of the country is to be found in the saddle and in the camp. It is not necessary to travel with such numbers and with such protection of authority as was our fortune. A smaller party, more independent of time and circumstances, is on many accounts even more desirable. If of men purely, four to eight is a fit number for an expedition; if the two sexes are combined, about double these limits will be found desirable. We met in the Middle Park a young man from Yale college, who was making a thorough journey of two months through the Mountains and Parks without any companions but such as he picked up from day to day or week to week. He had bought a pony and blankets and coffee-pot in Denver, and for the rest bargained for his daily rations en route, stopping for the night at ranches and hotels where he found them, and in cabins or tents, if the doors were open and there was room, and under a hospitable tree when all else was denied him.

August is the best month to come, for that is nearest summer in the high mountains; the streams are lower, purer and more readily forded; the weather most uniformly clear. But any time from June 15 to September 15 will answer for visiting either or both the great Parks; and I beg every "Across the Continent" traveler to give at least a week and if possible a month to the interior regions of Colorado. But do not come unless you will visit one of the Parks at least, go over one or two of the high passes, and ascend either Gray's Peak or Mount Lincoln. Else you will discredit my enthusiasm, and deny yourself when you talk of having seen Colorado.

pects of the communities through which he passes are always acute, in the great majority of cases original, and often profound. His descriptions of scenery are admirable, and he has the rare gift of knowing when he has given the reader enough of them. There is no other account of the Yo Semite Valley, or of the scenery and atmospheric effects of the plains and mountains and rivers of the Western Coast, which can at all compare to his. We cordially recommend everybody who wants a most valuable contribution to the social and political philosophy of the day, in the form of one of the most entertaining records of travel we have ever lighted upon, to buy and read this book. We have ourselves closed it with sincere regret that there was not more of it.

From the London Anglo-American Times.

Dr. Livingstone has written of equatorial Africa; Captain Speke of the Nile; Mr. Cameron of the Eastern Archipelago; and Madame Pfœffer of a voyage round the world; but no author, either English or foreign, has ever produced a book of travel of more absorbing interest than that now before us. It is certainly a remarkable book—remarkable not only for the clear insight it gives us of that immense and almost boundless region traversed by the writer, but for the charming ease, grace, and fluency with which he tells his story. We know something of the greatness of the American Republic, but we acknowledge that we never experienced so profound a sense of the unlimited resources, the boundless wealth, and the grand destiny of that country as we have done since reading this work. We advise all Americans who desire to know more of their own country, as well as all Englishmen who wish clear information regarding America, to peruse it.

From the San Francisco, Col., Bulletin.

As a record of travel it is admirable beyond praise. It is crowded with information, given in a style so fresh and piquant that even the most commonplace facts are made palatable. Mr. Bowles relates his experience so pleasantly, so genially, so free from the taint of snobbery and affectation, that it refreshes one to read him. He appears to be overrunning with vitality. His style is a model of graceful English—polished yet pointed—elegant, yet bristling with pith and antithesis.

From the Paris Correspondence of the New York Tribune.

See, in proof, that quintessentially American book of Samuel Bowles', the racy book of his letters, written *currente calamo*, "ACROSS THE CONTINENT." None but an American could have written it. None but a graduate of a New England school-house could have so written it; so vividly, so sympathetically, so artistically, even. Its classically literary defects are its realistic merits, regarded merely from the point of view of art. Verily, one need read that volume this side of the water to relish, to *sense* at their full quality, to appreciate with justly complete thankfulness, its special and eminent choice American bouquet.

From the Boston Advertiser.

Its striking descriptions of California life, of the wonders of Yo Semite Valley and of the Big Trees, of the noble charms of Oregon, and his appreciative observations on the growth of the national life among and beyond the Rocky Mountains, carry the reader in imagination into a region where all accustomed ideas and scenes seem poor by contrast. We have seen no discussion of the Mormon question which appears more sound, while there certainly is none more authentic and trustworthy.

By the Same Author.

THE HARTFORD PUBLISHING COMPANY issue in March, 1869—to be sold by subscription only—a fine large royal octavo volume of five hundred pages, combining the chief materials of "Across the Continent" and "Colorado: its Parks and Mountains," and much new and valuable matter,—entitled:—

Our New West.

RECORDS OF TRAVEL

BETWEEN THE MISSISSIPPI RIVER AND THE PACIFIC OCEAN.

OVER THE PLAINS—OVER THE MOUNTAINS—THROUGH THE GREAT INTERIOR BASIN—OVER THE SIERRA NEVADAS—TO AND UP AND DOWN THE PACIFIC COAST.

WITH

DETAILS OF THE WONDERFUL NATURAL SCENERY, AGRICULTURE, MINES, SOCIAL LIFE, PROGRESS AND PROSPECTS

OF

COLORADO, WYOMING, UTAH, IDAHO, MONTANA, NEVADA, CALIFORNIA, OREGON, WASHINGTON, AND BRITISH COLUMBIA;

Including the Mormons, the Indians, and the Chinese.

By SAMUEL BOWLES,

EDITOR OF THE SPRINGFIELD (MASS.) REPUBLICAN.

This volume will contain new steel engraved portraits of the author and his traveling companions, Vice-President Colfax, and Governor Bross; a comprehensive but complete Map; and sixteen full page illustrations of the scenery, the cities, and the characters described in the text,—all drawn and engraved expressly for this book.

The whole will present the most complete, graphic, authentic and freshly-drawn account, yet offered to the public, of Our New West of America, in which the opening of the Pacific Railroad has stimulated and spread so wide an interest.

The price of the volume—which is produced in the finest style of the typographic art—is $3.00. Persons wishing copies, or desiring to act as agents for its sale, will address the Publishers:—HARTFORD PUBLISHING CO., Hartford, Conn.; or, J. D. DENNISON, New York; or, J. A. STODDARD, Chicago, Ill.

Daily, Semi-Weekly, and Weekly.

The Springfield Republican,

A NEW ENGLAND FAMILY JOURNAL

OF

News, Politics, Literature and Social Life.

PUBLISHED BY

SAMUEL BOWLES & COMPANY,

SPRINGFIELD, MASS.

To picture the progress of the varied and busy life of New England, as to represent its inquisitive and active thought on all questions that concern the comfort and the elevation of society; to make, indeed, a part of that life and that thought, —this is the scope and aim of THE SPRINGFIELD REPUBLICAN newspaper. Confessedly it has become the most representative and comprehensive of New England journals; as a record of its news, for home use or foreign enlightenment; as an exponent of its best thought, most intelligent, candid and advanced, on questions of political and religious liberty and progress, of social order and development, and of literary and art culture;—and it is the ambition and effort of its conductors to maintain and extend this leadership, to still more elevate and widen the character of the paper, and to vary and enlarge its interest and usefulness for all classes of our people.

The prominent features of THE REPUBLICAN, as a Newspaper and Family Journal, are, completeness and promptness, intelligence and system in the preparation and publication of News of every description—seeking to give not only the fact but the meaning and moral of every event; free, candid and piquant Editorial Discussions of all public occurrences, men and things; intelligent and independent Correspondence from Boston, New York and Washington, the far West, and from Europe,—letters of travel, letters of fact, letters of opinion and criticism; Reviews and Extracts from New Books; special summaries of intelligence in the Literary, Art and Religious worlds; Stories, Sketches, Essays, Poetry, bits of Biography, Science, Agriculture, Mechanics, etc., from original contributors, or from the choicest magazines and literary journals of America and Europe. No other newspaper proper gives so much space as THE REPUBLICAN to all this latter wide variety of Literary and Family Reading. DR. J. G. HOLLAND (Timothy Titcomb) is writing letters from Europe for THE REPUBLICAN; and "WARRINGTON" (W. S. Robinson) contributes regularly to its columns from Boston.

THE WEEKLY REPUBLICAN is becoming more and more a general Family Political, Social and Literary Journal. Its full and intelligent Review of the Week, its page of especial New England items, and its two columns of financial, commercial and market affairs furnish its readers all that is wanting in the way of news. Especial events are given in more detail. But the great bulk of its ample pages are devoted to Editorial Discussions, Correspondence, Literary Reviews and Selections, Stories and Essays, and other interesting and instructive family reading. Its circulation is rapidly extending, not only throughout New England, but all over the country; first, as the best compiler of local New England news; second, as the best representative of nationalized New England opinion; and, third, as a generous collection of the best current literature of the day.

THE DAILY REPUBLICAN is published three times a week, and the SEMI-WEEKLY and WEEKLY, regularly, on a large double sheet of eight pages and 48 columns. Their circulation is unprecedented in the history of provincial journalism. No papers out of the largest cities have so large or wide-spread a reading. This enables the proprietors to afford the several issues at prices as low as any and lower than most of its contemporaries. While most first-class daily newspapers are sold at four and five cents a copy and $10 and $12 a year, THE DAILY REPUBLICAN is furnished at three cents and $8 a year; THE SEMI-WEEKLY at $4 a year, or $3 in clubs; and THE WEEKLY at $2, or $1.75 in clubs.

www.ingramcontent.com/pod-product-compliance
Lightning Source LLC
Chambersburg PA
CBHW031116020726
47495CB00007B/2220